LUKE BALDWIN'S VOW

MORLEY CALLAGHAN

Stoddart Kids

*We acknowledge the Canada Council for the Arts and the
Ontario Arts Council for their support of our publishing program.*

A GEMINI BOOK

First published in 1945 by Macmillan of Canada,
a division of Canada Publishing Corporation.

Published in 1995 by Stoddart Publishing Co. Limited

Published in 1997 by Stoddart Kids,
a division of Stoddart Publishing Co. Limited
34 Lesmill Road
Toronto, Canada M3B 2T6
Tel. (416) 445-3333 Fax (416) 445-5967
E-mail Customer.Service@ccmailgw.genpub.com

Canadian Cataloguing in Publication Data

Callaghan, Morley, 1903–1990
Luke Baldwin's vow

ISBN: 0-7736-7440-3

I. Title.
PS8505.A43L8 1995   jC813'.52   C95-931252-8

Cover Design: Bill Douglas/The Bang
Cover Illustration: David Craig

Printed and bound in Canada

Contents

1. The Separation

THAT morning in the second week of May when it was raining so hard, Dr. Baldwin got a call from old Mrs. Wilson. It was her third call in two days, and the doctor's housekeeper, Mrs. Jackson, a gray-haired, thin, gruff woman, said tartly, "Doctor, you know as well as I do there's nothing the matter with that woman. She's seventy-nine years old and she'd have you holding her hand every time she coughs a little. You've been out twice during the night and it's raining cats and dogs now. Why don't you get some sleep and let Mrs. Wilson wait?"

But the doctor, chuckling as if he liked being scolded by his housekeeper, winked at Luke, who was sitting there at the breakfast table with him.

"Why, the poor woman may be dying," he said. "And besides, she's been counting on me all these years. Isn't that right, Luke?"

"Yeah, that's right," the doctor's son said.

"So out into the rain I go," the doctor said cheerfully with the slow easy smile his son liked so much. A thin dark man with a gentle, scholarly face, he was careless with his accounts and yet took an extraordinary interest in the petty ailments of his patients. His scolding housekeeper often insisted that he should have married again and got a wife who would have taken a sensible interest in his affairs. Yet she really would have hated to see a sensible woman there in the house twisting and ordering the doctor's life around.

So that morning the doctor put on his raincoat and his old brown felt hat and went out to his car, which he had left parked in front of his house all night.

Luke, who had gone to the front window, watched his father stand for a moment in the heavy rain. When himself grew older, Luke wanted to have his father's easy relaxed manner and his quiet strength. Even now people said he looked like his father, though he was fair and slight and small for his age and his blue eyes were a bit too serious. In some ways he was old for his age because he spent so much time with his father, but in other ways, particularly when he was with bigger and rougher boys, he seemed young and reticent.

There at the window he waited to see the car pull away before he got ready to go to school. But the doctor seemed to have trouble starting the car. The starter spun, and spun again, and then spun steadily for almost a minute. The battery weakened, and soon the slow heavy spin was hardly turning the engine over.

Then the doctor got out of the car and stood in the rain with his hands in his pockets. Turning, he looked at the window and shrugged and grinned at Luke. After he had lifted the hood and peered in at the engine, he turned again to the window with the same slow smile.

Luke waved his hand encouragingly, for the doctor had been able to make him believe they should always encourage each other. It was as if they had the one life in common; whenever they were together, whether they were fishing on a week end or talking for an hour at night before Luke went to bed, they were able to talk as if they were at one time two boys and at another time two men.

And the doctor there in the rain, looking thoughtfully at the car and then again at the window, finally came to a decision; he made motions with his hand to Luke, who opened the window.

"Hey, son, how would you like to put on your raincoat and come out here for a minute?" he called.

"Sure I will," Luke said eagerly. Getting his raincoat he hurried out. "What is it, Dad?" he asked.

"Luke, you get in the car there in the front seat," the doctor said. "I'm going to have you help me start the car."

"Okay," Luke said quickly. He was excited and a little afraid and yet was full of eagerness. Many times he had sat in the front seat working the gears, and his father had promised that when Luke's legs got long enough to reach the pedals he would let him really start the car. He was too small now to push down the brake or press the accelerator without shoving himself down behind the wheel, and knowing this, his father got into the car beside him, released the clutch, put the car in gear and turned on the ignition. "Here's all I want you to do, Luke," he said, with his easy smile that always gave Luke confidence. "Keep your foot pressed down on the clutch, and when I yell, lift your foot off. Understand? You see, son, if I push the car just ten feet or so we're on the hill, then the car will roll down itself and start. I'll jump in. Understand?"

"Okay, it'll be easy," Luke said. Once before Luke had seen his father start the car in this way. But that other day his father had called out to a sixteen-year-old boy across the street and Luke had been disappointed that he himself had been considered too small to help his father.

Now Luke sat proudly behind the wheel, hoping neighbors would be watching at their windows. All that made him nervous was that the rain blurred the windshield even though the wipers were swinging back and forth. The glistening street looked slippery. In the steadily falling rain nothing seemed to be quite normal. The rain splashed on the car and on the doctor's hunched-up shoulders as he stood beside the car, one strong hand on the door handle, leaning his weight and pushing, his feet slipping a little as the car hardly moved. Resting, he wiped the rain off his face with his handkerchief and then began to push again.

The car moved a little and Luke, staring raptly down the slope, his hands tight on the wheel, his heart pounding, heard his father gasping for breath. But the front wheels were getting a little closer to the edge of the slope. The gasping became a little louder; the car was no longer moving. One strange gasp had come from the doctor as Luke waited. Then he thought he heard a whisper, "Luke," from down near the wheels. When he turned and couldn't see his father he got scared. Taking his foot off the clutch he yelled, "Aren't you pushing, dad? It isn't moving at all."

When his father didn't answer, Luke jumped out and there was his father sitting in a pool of water beside the back wheel, with one leg hooked under him and the other leg, the right one, stretched out stiffly. The wet hat had fallen off his head. The gray-black hair was wet and matted and raindrops were streaming down his gray wet face. His eyes were closed but his lips were moving. "Get someone, Luke," he whispered, and then his head sagged back against the wheel of the car.

Screaming "Mrs. Jackson! Oh, please hurry, Mrs. Jackson!" Luke ran toward the house.

Mrs. Jackson came out in her white apron, crying, "Oh, dear!" As she raised her hands to her head she knocked off her glasses and stumbled around in a circle. Luke picked up the glasses for her, but they were wet and muddied and she had to wipe them on her apron. Then she hurried into the house next door, and Mr. Hunter, a plump man, a lawyer, came out and with another neighbor, Mr. Willenski, carried Dr. Baldwin into the house while Mrs. Jackson phoned for another doctor.

The old doctor who lived three blocks away and who came within twenty minutes said that Dr. Baldwin had had a heart attack. This doctor made disgusted clucking noises with his tongue, and he said to Mrs. Jackson as he stood in the hall putting on his coat, "To push a car. What a foolish gesture for any man his age. I can't understand it. It's simply irrational."

Now that Dr. Baldwin had regained consciousness and was safe in his own bed Mrs. Jackson was more at ease. "He's the best-hearted man on this earth, is the doctor," she muttered. "But so utterly unpractical. Now why should he have wasted his time bothering to see that silly old Mrs. Wilson? I told him not to bother."

Luke, who had been listening, scowled, for he didn't like the way she was talking about his father, and he didn't like this old doctor's superior tone, and it seemed to him they were trying to make themselves important by making a fuss over his father.

Nor did he like it when Aunt Helen, who was the wife of his father's brother, came that night to stay with them for a few days. Her husband, Uncle Henry, who had a saw-mill just outside Collingwood on the Georgian Bay, had insisted she stay with them both until Luke's father was much better.

Not that Aunt Helen wasn't a kind and friendly woman, but she knew too well exactly what should be done, and to Luke she was a stranger in the house. Aunt Helen had a bright bustling cheerful manner. She was a small plump woman with brown hair and a glowing pink skin, and a pink throat and plump hands, and she smelled of freshly laundered clothes and sensible soap, and she soon had old Mrs. Jackson hustling around the house and muttering glumly to herself.

The next Thursday Dr. Baldwin had another heart attack, which came suddenly when he was sitting up in the bed.

From that time on Luke knew that his father was expected to die. He knew it because two other doctors who had come to the house whispered together and looked grave, and Mrs. Jackson hurrying to her room with Luke tiptoeing after her had wept quietly on her bed, and Luke listening at her door had felt bewildered. Mrs. Jackson had always seemed like a stern scolding sensible woman who would never cry. When she came out of the room she put her arms around him. It frightened him. Other little things also began to convince Luke, and he would whisper to himself stupidly, "They think Dad is dying," as if he were getting used to the sound of the word, which had no meaning for him; he couldn't imagine that his father would ever really die and go away from him.

In these days of loneliness Luke wanted companionship more than anything; but he wanted a kind of companionship these women could not offer him. He found himself longing again for Mike, the little Irish terrier—Mike, who had been killed by a milk wagon only three months ago. Luke's father had wanted to get him another dog at once, but Luke would not let him. He had believed they were only trying to make him forget his own dog.

So he kept to himself while Aunt Helen sent telegrams and whispered endlessly with Mrs. Jackson. And sometimes he asked, "Why can't I talk to my father?" "Be a good boy, Luke," Aunt Helen said. That was all she would say and Luke was angry. It was good to be able to feel angry.

Only the doctors went into the bedroom until the last day; then Aunt Helen, looking flustered and unhappy in her new brown dress, was permitted to talk to her brother-in-law. As Luke waited in his own room he didn't like the lonely call of the nighthawks swooping among the trees and the chimneys of the houses. So he walked along the hall to his father's room. In his imagination he could see every detail of the room, the big chair by the window, the carved mahogany bed that had belonged to his grandmother and the bureau, hand-carved and mahogany too; thinking of these familiar things, seeing them so clearly in his mind, made him feel better.

The young doctor from the hospital, who was very precise and clean and who looked like a smart young businessman in his double-breasted gray suit, came out of the bedroom and took Luke by the arm.

"Luke," he said in a confidential tone as if they were both the same age, "your father wants to have a little talk with you. He's asked for you. It must be a very little talk, Luke. Understand? A big fellow like you will know how to take it easy, eh?"

"Yes, sir," Luke said.

"Come on now, son," the young doctor said and he led Luke into the bedroom.

But the familiar things in the bedroom all ceased to be familiar as soon as Luke entered the room. His father didn't turn his head. Aunt Helen and the doctor remained there, and Luke, in a trance, moved close to the bed, not looking unhappy or scared, but with a fixed polite smile on his face to assure them all that nothing could jar him. But his father's hand was on the bed cover and when Luke saw the hand he stared at it blankly. He touched it timidly. "Hello, Dad," he said.

"Luke, son," his father said, his blue eyes opening and yet hardly seeing; turning his head a little, his eyes now surprisingly clear and calm, he tried to speak and had difficulty with his breathing. "Luke," he said. "Luke." His fingers clutched at the boy's hand. There was a slight twist of his lips as if the grin Luke loved was hovering around his lips. The memory of all the little things they did together, the long walks they took together, the evenings a few years ago when his father read to him at bedtime, the explanations about the world, the legends told again and again, and the agreement that the world was bright and mysterious and not to be easily understood, all was offered to Luke in that twitching little smile. It was more immediate and more real to Luke than this scene in the bedroom; it was like a secret knowledge of his father's strength. It had far more reality than the troubled face of Aunt Helen who waited so stiffly, or the alert and certain knowledge possessed by the young doctor who was watching at the foot of the bed. All Luke's life with his father was dancing swiftly through his mind; a life which they shared and which he believed could never be broken. So he waited with his frightened little smile.

"Luke, son," his father went on slowly. "I may be leaving you for a little while. It's just like going away...going a little farther away...but I'm there, Luke. Do you see, son?"

"Sure, Daddy," Luke whispered.

"I want you to go and live with Aunt Helen and your Uncle Henry. He's a fine man, Luke, and kind, too, and he'll look after you. A small town is a great place for a boy. You go with them, Luke."

"Yes, but not now, Dad," Luke protested.

"No, in a little while, son."

"Yeah, a little while."

"And Luke," the voice came more slowly now, coming from farther away and with a more painful effort, "I want you to learn things from Uncle Henry. All kinds of things about the world. Learn from him and remember. Will you, Luke?"

"Yes, I will, Dad. I'll learn from Uncle Henry."

"No one will have to worry about you then," the doctor whispered and he tried to move his head; his eyes did shift to his brother's wife, who nodded quickly. A faint smile was on the doctor's face. "Henry knew how to handle things, always did, didn't he, Helen?" he whispered.

"Of course, of course," she said quickly.

After a long pause Dr. Baldwin whispered, "Luke, are you still there?"

"I'm here, Daddy."

"I'll never be far away from you, son. Here and there... not far away." He sighed and his breathing became very difficult. The young doctor motioned to Aunt Helen to take Luke away.

Then he was standing by the door of the living room where his aunt and Mrs. Jackson were talking in low tones.

He didn't like the way Mrs. Jackson's face broke into heavy twitching frowns. It scared him. Her eyes were glazed and moist, and because she was trying not to cry as they whispered, she looked extraordinarily stern.

Not knowing that both these women longed to offer him a comforting motherly tenderness, he eyed them uneasily. Mrs. Jackson, her voice breaking a little, said, "Come here, Luke," and as he approached slowly she blurted out impulsively, "Oh, Luke, you're like my own son, oh, my boy, my boy."

And Aunt Helen, her own eyes filling, stood up suddenly. "Luke...son, son," she whispered, and though she never had a son of her own and had never particularly wanted children, she longed to embrace Luke because he was losing his father and would be alone; her feeling of motherly tenderness was so strange to her that she swallowed hard and couldn't speak.

Luke was surprised more than anything else at the way his aunt's throat trembled, and the way her chin jerked.

"Come here, Luke," she pleaded.

"Why?" he asked, drawing back suspiciously.

"Oh, God bless you, Luke. Never mind," Mrs. Jackson said gently. She too stood up and tried to put her arms around Luke, but he pushed her away almost fiercely. "What's the matter with you?" he asked in a worried tone. "Why don't you leave me alone?"

He stood as he often stood, his hands straight at his sides, his wide, blue, steady eyes watchful, a lock of fair hair low on his forehead, looking as if he were ready to fight or run, yet feeling only a desperate resentment against them. It was as if they were suddenly trying to take somebody else's place in his life.

"My poor boy, what's the matter?" Aunt Helen asked, growing bewildered because of the resentment in his eyes.

"Nothing's the matter," he protested desperately. "Why do you go on as if something's the matter?" he asked. As her arms came out to him and his head was held against her bosom he could smell the powder she used. Squirming away he protested, "Leave me alone. I'm all right." He sounded angry and bewildered and the two women looked at each other helplessly.

Again Luke had the feeling that Mike ought to have been with him, that he needed Mike especially now. A dog knows how to share your bewilderment and sadness without getting in the way; he knows how to sit beside you quietly without asking any recognition.

He went out and sat down on the front steps and watched some bigger boys passing on the other side of the darkening street. "Hi," he called mechanically. "Hi, Luke," they answered in a tone which worried him. The nighthawk swooping over the house uttered its loud screeching complaint, and the cry suddenly bewildered him. All day he had been confused because nothing that had been happening seemed to have any reality. He knew he was expected to be alone. Yet he did not really believe he was to be alone.

At four o'clock in the morning his father died and when they told Luke he did not cry. He still couldn't believe in his father's death. He felt amazement more than anything.

2. An Old Dog &
A Sensible Uncle

W HEN Luke got off the train at the Collingwood station that afternoon he looked around uneasily, wondering what this place was to mean in his life. Carrying his bag and wearing his best gray suit, he walked slowly along the station platform looking at the wide smooth water of the blue bay and at the horizon where a ship's smoke trailed into a thin wisp and where rolling white clouds piled up into great vaulted cathedrals against the blue sky. To the north beyond the little station and the rows of houses were hills with farms, hills rising into a range of wonderfully blue mountains such as he had never seen before. Those mountains began to fascinate him and he relaxed a little. From the other side of the station came the whirring and pounding of drills on metal. Great steel beams rose against the sky. This was the shipyard. The hull of a vessel was there amid the steel network. Men suspended on little swinging seats pounded away at the steel plates. To the right was the long pier with the white grain elevator, and tied up at the pier was a ship loading grain.

In those days Collingwood was a town of seven thousand, where the men worked overtime in the shipyard and the dry-dock, for the grain boats came to the elevator from the northern lakes and from Chicago and Cleveland. And the town was built around the harbor and the shore line, and then there were the hills and the farms extending up to the blue mountains.

"Luke, oh, Luke," cried his Aunt Helen, "here I am," and she came hurrying along the station platform in her gray spring coat and her neat little blue hat. Her short plump legs seemed to be full of energy. Her bright round face was beaming. She offered him a warm welcome. And he offered to her the apologetic eager shyness of a boy who knew now he had no home of his own. Taking his bag and chattering cheerfully, she led him to the car and drove away from the station, going south on the dusty gravel road which twisted and turned following the line of the bay.

"Ah, Luke," she said warmly, for she was far too sensible a woman to be embarrassed by a boy's shyness, "you're going to have a fine time around the sawmill with your Uncle Henry. An intelligent boy like you growing up around our place is just the ticket for your uncle, Luke."

"I don't remember Uncle Henry very well, Aunt Helen."

"Why should you? You haven't seen him for years. But

you'll take to him, and he'll always be there to give you a hand. No matter how busy he is."

"Is Uncle Henry very busy?" Luke asked politely.

"Oh, yes, your Uncle Henry is a man who can't bear to be idle. There's always something doing when he's around. What are you looking at, Luke?"

"At the lake. Are those clouds?" he asked, pointing to heavy white clouds low on the water line which seemed to have strange depths like caverns or mountain valleys. "Or are they islands?"

"There's an island over there," she said. "Christian Island, an Indian reservation, Luke. It's a legendary spot."

"What's a legendary spot, Aunt Helen?"

"A spot where tragic things happened to people a long time ago," she said. "Yes, I think that's how you'd describe it."

A long time ago a band of Indians had retreated to that island and had held it against a more powerful tribe, she explained as the car passed the last of the outlying houses with single cows grazing in the fields. Ahead was the mouth of a river, and there the road turned. They followed this tree-lined river a few hundred yards, and there was the building which had served as a sawmill for over a hundred years. It had a big stone foundation with red clapboard, and a mill pond and a dam and a fine abandoned moss-covered water wheel. There were piles of lumber and one great pile of sawdust at the back of a low red brick building. Across the river was the thick woods rising like green mounds which were wooded hills. And the air was filled with the wild screeching sound of great saws hacking through the logs in the mill.

To the right, and well back from the mill, was a three-story house, the woodwork freshly painted white and green and with a green veranda. "Come on, Luke. Here we are," Aunt Helen said. When he got out of the car he stood for a moment looking solemnly up at the roof of the house, then he looked at the sawmill, and as he turned to follow his aunt a dog which had been lying in the shade at the corner of the house came toward him slowly.

He was an old collie with an amber-colored coat and one fine amber-colored eye. The other eye was blind. The left hind leg had a limp in it. No one had brushed or combed out the amber-colored fur.

The collie saw Luke and stopped apprehensively, for the boy was a stranger. And Luke turned, and then they were both staring at each other.

The dog's black nose twitched a little; he flopped his tail back and forth in slow speculation. As Luke watched and wondered the collie dipped his head, took a few steps toward Luke, then lifted his head with what was almost a gesture of recognition, and wagged his tail again.

"Where did you come from, mister?" Luke said.

The dog kept wagging his heavy tail and sniffing, then he stopped all motion, looking up at Luke with that strange expression of recognition.

"Well, hello, mister. You look as if you were waiting here for me," Luke said. Dropping on his knees he said, "Come on, put your paw up."

As if he were fumbling for a forgotten motion, the collie slowly raised his right paw and they shook hands. Luke began to stroke his head, and this meeting with the old dog brought relief that was like happiness. "Wait awhile, will you, and I'll see you later," he said, for his aunt was calling from the hall.

Hurrying in, he followed her up to the attic to the room that was to be his, a clean white room with a newly purchased serviceable iron bed, a new chest of drawers, a new hooked rug on the floor, and on the wall an etching of an English cathedral. Bright chintz curtains were on the window that overlooked the bay. But Luke hardly looked around. It was just another strange room to him.

"I know you'll be a clean neat boy, Luke," his aunt said brightly as she began unpacking his clothes and hanging them neatly in the closet. "And always hang your things up. Of course a lot of these things you have here won't be suitable for playing and going to school in the country. First you'll need a heavy pair of shoes."

"Aunt Helen, about that dog," he said.

"You mean Dan. What about Dan?"

"Well, for one thing, he had the kindest face I ever saw on a dog."

"Yes, Dan's a nice old dog," she said casually. "I sometimes forget he's around here, I'm so used to him. And he's been around here so long."

"Is he a thoroughbred?"

"Yes, he's a thoroughbred, though you'd never believe it now."

"What do you use him for?"

"Nothing, Luke. Nothing at all. He's on a pension, you might say. Oh, you're going to like it around here, Luke. Swimming in the river and romping in the woods. Do you know something, Luke, before you were born your father used to come up here and hunt with your uncle in the woods across the river."

"Oh!"

"Yes, he certainly did. I can remember those times well," she said with a sigh as she held a pair of his pants in her two hands, and forgot she was holding them. "Yes, I was just married, and Uncle Henry was just starting to get along. Yet I knew he'd get along. I knew from the beginning, Luke. If you want to grow up and get along and learn how to handle people, you just keep your eye on your uncle, Luke."

"Yes, that's what my father said," he agreed, frowning doubtfully.

"Oh, he knew. Your father knew he was giving you splendid advice, Luke. And you'll learn too."

"But, Aunt Helen..."

"What, Luke?"

"Just what is it I'm to learn from Uncle Henry?"

"Why, that's a funny question," she said in astonishment. "Doesn't somebody have to show a boy how to live in this world?" Her faith in her husband was so splendid that it had never occurred to her that he wouldn't be able to arrange Luke's life for him as he had arranged her life for her. She had an easy comfortable life. Everything was always in the right place. With Uncle Henry around she never had to sit down and worry about which places were the right places. Having no children of her own she had wondered if having a boy in the house might upset her a little, but Uncle Henry had assured her that Luke would adjust himself perfectly to their ways and it didn't occur to her to doubt his word. "What are these?" she asked, remembering she was holding his pants in her hands. "Oh, yes, your pants." But suddenly she sniffed and grew concerned. "I believe I smell the roast. Oh, dear," she cried. "I put it in the oven before I went to the station."

Hurrying down to her kitchen with Luke following her, she opened the oven, drew out the pan and stuck a fork in the beef with a loving concern. "Uncle Henry can't stand it if the roast is cooked too much," she explained. "Thank heavens it isn't overdone. You go out and look around, Luke."

When he went out Luke was surprised to find the dog waiting at the foot of the steps. The dog was not sleeping or resting there; he was really waiting. "Come on, boy," Luke said, and the dog trailed after him with a slow ambling gait.

First they stood at the edge of the mill pond gazing toward the bush where, according to Aunt Helen, Luke's father had often hunted with Uncle Henry, and the bush looked dark and cool and he began to rub his hand through his hair, frowning and trying to understand why he felt such a compulsion to plunge into the bush at once. The impulse troubled him. But gradually the whine of the saw hacking through logs began to distract him, for the sound, like an agonized shriek which he had never heard before, rose and died and rose again, and he went closer to the entrance of the mill. He wanted to see without being seen, and he stopped by a small window near the door. All around the entrance was sawdust spreading out like a gold cloth, and when he walked on this sawdust it was like walking noiselessly on a thick golden carpet.

While Luke stood on his toes trying to look in the window, the dog flopped down on the sawdust about ten feet away from him and waited.

Then an elderly man, in blue overalls, with coarse gray hair, a heavy gray unevenly clipped beard and a slow shuffling gait came out of the mill carrying a long two by four scantling. He was Sam Carter, who had worked for Uncle Henry for ten years without missing a day. He lived alone in a rough cast cottage a half mile along the road to town and never talked with his neighbors and never went anywhere in the company of another man. He had never been married, never drank, never spent much money, needed little to live on. He was an excellent workman but no one had ever heard him laugh out loud. He was not an unhappy man, but the only kind of happiness he had ever known came from doing exactly what he was told to do.

In Sam Carter's face there was something heavy, slow and dull. It was a deeply tanned impassive face incapable of showing any emotion. The eyes were deep-set, old and wrathful with an expression of resignation that never changed.

Luke, who had never seen such a man, gaped at him as if wondering where he had come from and watched him carrying the scantling, stopping a little, and shifting the weight of the scantling in his thick brown hands. As Sam Carter made a turn he did not see the dog and his boot touched his tail; with a yelp the collie jumped up.

Then Sam Carter turned back and spat and kicked mechanically at the dog as if it wasn't very important whether the heavy boot was buried in the dog's ribs, or whether the boot missed the dog, and so the thick boot only grazed Dan's flank as he swerved away.

"Hey!" Luke cried indignantly. "Don't do that."

"Uh?" said Sam Carter.

"That's my Uncle Henry's dog," Luke said sharply.

"Uh, yeah," Sam Carter said. Neither abashed nor angry nor apologetic, he stared at the boy with the fair hair and the candid blue eyes which were now so angry. He seemed to be letting a picture of the boy form in his mind, and yet he still did not seem to be completely aware that the boy was there. After a moment's pondering he decided that nothing had been said or nothing important enough had happened to compel his recognition of the fact that the boy was there. So he turned away and tramped heavily along the path with his scantling.

"Who does he think he is around here?" Luke whispered to Dan. "Wait till Uncle Henry hears that guy kicked at you." His fists were clenched and his heart was pounding. But with a flash of insight he thought, "It was the way he kicked at him. As if it wasn't important, as if Dan had no right to be around here getting in the way. A man like that working for Uncle Henry wouldn't kick Uncle Henry's dog if he knew the dog was important to Uncle Henry." And this thought saddened him.

Old Sam Carter, returning with the same shuffling stride, still looking at Luke, yet way beyond him and still giving no recognition to the fact that Luke was there, turned into the mill. Sam Carter's vast, calm, slow imperviousness frightened him. It had all happened quickly, it was only a little thing, but now Luke understood that Dan had no importance around the mill. Even the workmen understood that Uncle Henry was no longer concerned about what happened to the dog.

"Come here, Dan," he said, and bending down he began to stroke the dog's head gently. "Don't you worry, Dan," he said. "You're my pal, understand?"

But then there was one slow whine from the mill as the saws stopped whirling and a sudden astonishing silence overwhelmed the mill, the river and the woods. This silence was finally broken by the voices of the men quitting work. And Uncle Henry himself came striding out of the mill.

He was a big burly man weighing more than two hundred and thirty pounds and he had a rough-skinned, brick-colored face. On his head was a straw hat pushed well back, in his mouth an unlighted cigar and he had on a spotlessly clean shirt with the sleeves rolled up. His brown forearms were mottled with freckles. He wore a dark blue tie. An expensive wrist watch was on his left wrist. And Luke looked at him with a shy apprehensiveness, for this was the man from whom his father expected him to learn so much.

"Hello there, my boy," Uncle Henry called out heartily. "Why didn't you come right in and see me?"

"I thought you might be busy," Luke said shyly.

"Sure, I was busy, Luke," Uncle Henry said, putting his big hand on Luke's shoulder and leading him along with him toward the house. "But you could have been busy with me. Never mind. I can see you've been looking around getting the lay of the land. Well, that's the stuff." He was jolly and friendly, his manner straightforward, his voice rich, deep and hearty. He was completely at ease. But Luke, who was accustomed to his father's lazy, indirect gentleness and slow smile couldn't quite get used to Uncle Henry.

"What do you say if we wash up together?" Uncle Henry said. "You know, Luke," he went on. "Just yesterday I was talking about you to the principal of the school. A nice school. They'll be glad to have you. I said you'd want to plunge right in. That's right, isn't it? No use giving yourself a chance to notice any break with things as you knew them in the city. Understand, son? Plunge right in with a good heart."

He sounded as if he had it all figured out, and indeed he had, too, for Uncle Henry was a man who liked to accept responsibility. When he had realized that he was going to have the responsibility of rearing his dead brother's boy he had gravely considered all that was involved. Being a practical man he liked working according to a plan. His brother, the doctor, had gone to college, but Uncle Henry, who had only a high school education, was proud of the way he had trained his own mind and the success he had made out of life. A boy like Luke was to have the advantage of his experience. A boy should grow up to be sensible, shrewd, clear-thinking, hard-headed, with an instinctive knowledge of what was useful in the world and what was false, sentimental and unnecessary. In the last week Uncle Henry had read three books on child psychology. In one of these books he had found paragraphs that he had read aloud to his wife with approval. "This man at least offers a glimmer of common sense," he had said. "And I know it's good sense because it checks with my own experience."

But as Uncle Henry walked along, exuding confidence and authority, Luke drew away shyly trying to figure him out. He knew Uncle Henry was being kind to him, and yet he kept asking himself how it was that a man so eager to be kind and friendly could be indifferent to what happened to a fine old dog like Dan. It might be that Uncle Henry didn't believe the dog was important to anybody. Maybe if Uncle Henry could see that Dan was important to him, Luke, then Dan might become important again to Uncle Henry. He suddenly felt closer to Uncle Henry.

Chatting cheerfully they washed up together and Uncle Henry asked him how he liked his room, and when they were drying their hands he said he would go up to the room then and see if it looked like a satisfactory boy's room now Luke was in it. After he had inspected the attic room carefully and had examined all Luke's extra clothing, he decided that a satisfactory boy's room ought to have a desk at the window where a boy could study alone and undisturbed. "Yes, a desk by all means," he said, and taking a little black book from his hip pocket he said aloud as he wrote carefully, "One desk to go by window in Luke's room. Get it tomorrow.

"Books. Ah, I see you're a reader, Luke," he said, pointing to the bureau where Aunt Helen had laid the two books Luke had brought with him. "What's this one?" he asked, picking up the pirate story of days on the Spanish Main. "H-m. A pirate story." Then he began making regretful little clucking noises in his throat. "Aren't you a little old for that kind of stuff, Luke?"

But the collection of fairy stories by Hans Andersen really disturbed him. His smile wasn't indulgent; it was regretful and pitying, as if he were wondering whether he should say anything at the moment. "H-m, I see. Fairy tales. Do you like fairy tales, Luke?"

"I've read that book twice, Uncle Henry," Luke said proudly.

"I see. And did your father like your reading fairy tales?"

"Oh, sure, Uncle Henry. When I was small he used to read them to me."

"That surprises me, Luke," Uncle Henry said frankly, as he sat down on the edge of the bed. "Yes, it really does," he added, pondering the matter gravely.

"Why does it surprise you, Uncle Henry?"

"Your father was an educated man, Luke."

"He certainly was."

"Tell me, Luke, did you grow up believing in Santa Claus, too?"

"I sure did," Luke said with a grin, for he thought his uncle was kidding him.

"And suddenly there was no Santa Claus, eh?" Uncle Henry asked with a shrug.

"Oh, I just grew out of it."

"I wonder, I really wonder," Uncle Henry said half to himself.

"Wonder what, Uncle Henry?"

"Does a boy ever grow out of it?" Uncle Henry asked sadly. Luke knew then that his uncle was not kidding. "You're a sincere boy, Luke," he went on, his deep voice taking on a tone of persuasive authority. "I like a boy to be sincere. I like a man to be sincere. Sincere and mature."

"Sincere and mature. Yeah," Luke said.

"Sit down, Luke, and I'll try and explain. After all, this is important and I'm glad the subject came up," he said, looking at the book he held in both hands. "Come on, sit down beside me, Luke."

Bewildered by his uncle's grave tone, and with his eyes on the book which suddenly seemed to become something lewd and vulgar, Luke sat down apprehensively beside his uncle.

"I don't know if your father gave much time to such things," Uncle Henry said deprecatingly. "Of course a lot depends on the kind of man he wanted you to be. I take it he wanted you to be sincere and mature..."

"What's wrong with that book, Uncle Henry?"

"Fairy stories. What's wrong with fairy stories? Well, that's a fair question, Luke," he said briskly, for he was on a subject that was dear to his heart and on which he believed he held the soundest of all opinions. "What I'm going to say, Luke," he went on solemnly, "has the support of the most progressive minds in the whole world." With a sudden clearing of his throat he asked, "My boy, what would you say is the matter with the world?"

"I don't know," Luke said, looking puzzled. "Up until a while ago I didn't think there was much wrong with it."

"Naturally, naturally. Yes, but you know that history has always been a mess. People have always been fools, Luke. People have crazy, twisted minds, Luke. They're afraid of each other and afraid of being alive. Afraid of the world, Luke. Understand?"

"Well..."

"Of course you don't understand."

"No, I guess I don't."

"I'm going to tell you why everybody gets so mixed up, Luke. Now's the time, when I have this book here in my hands, eh? Here's what's the matter with the world and most of the people in it. They like telling lies to each other. Do you see?"

"I don't tell lies, Uncle Henry," Luke said guardedly. He didn't know what was coming, but he felt that an assault was being made upon him and something important was going to be taken away from him.

"Luke," Uncle Henry said, warming up and emphasizing his argument with emphatic gestures with his big right fist, "you have the root of the whole trouble right here in this fairy book. What is it? Simply lies. For thousands of years men have loved to tell lies to each other about the world. Isn't that awful, Luke? And worse still, mind you, they have loved to tell lies to their children. Why, Luke, your young head at this moment is probably full of lies."

"Yeah, I guess it is," Luke said, in the same guarded watchful tone. "Only... only what lies, Uncle Henry?"

"That's good. A good question, my boy. Well, people make up silly sentimental legends and myths to explain things to children. Listen, Luke, were you ever told there was a man in the moon?"

"Well, I guess, I mean..." Luke nodded, feeling ashamed and embarrassed. "I used to think I could see the man in the moon. Only I know now there isn't a man in the moon, Uncle Henry."

"And was thunder supposed to come when an angry god pounded on his shield, my boy? Oh, sure, sure. And a rainbow, I suppose, is a promise of something good about to happen! How in the world are you going to adjust yourself later on in real life if you believe these myths? You see the danger, Luke?"

"What's the danger, Uncle Henry?" Luke asked, deeply impressed by Uncle Henry's high seriousness.

"All your life you could go on being dreamy, Luke. I think you may be a little dreamy now. Your life could be so unhappy always reaching for consoling lies, superstitious and ignorant lies. Ah, no, Luke, get into the hard bright world. Face the facts, Luke. Always the facts. Understand?"

"I think I do," Luke said gravely. While they nodded solemnly to each other he was suddenly trying to grasp the fact that millions of people for thousands of years had been mixing each other up with lies and illusions and superstitions and doing all kinds of crazy things to each other—all because they were afraid to live in Uncle Henry's clear bright world; he tried to grasp the enormity of this tragedy but couldn't because he didn't believe in it.

"Don't worry, Luke," Uncle Henry consoled him as he smiled and stood up with the book, which Luke was never to see again, still under his arm. "We'll look after you. You'll soon get a good practical view of things, Luke."

"That'll be swell, Uncle Henry."

"When I was a boy I read biographies," Uncle Henry said, leading the way downstairs. "Good useful biographies. Nothing but biographies. Read about men like Ford and Edison. Splendid useful lives. We've got a library there in town, Luke. I'll get you a card."

As he followed his uncle downstairs Luke had his eye on the book, which was still tucked under Uncle Henry's arm. And it wasn't that he minded losing the book, for he had read it twice anyway, but he felt that something else was being taken away from him, something he needed which he couldn't define right then, but which was the splendor and insight of the imagination.

3. An Easy Understanding

I<small>T</small> was hard for Luke to feel at home at the dinner table. Aunt Helen talked all the time and Uncle Henry's authoritative personality seemed to intimidate him, and for another thing, Luke did not understand the language they were using, even though he understood every single word. He wanted to hide his shyness and his loneliness. When Uncle Henry had gone out to the veranda to smoke his cigar, Luke asked his aunt if he could take the dog up to his room.

There he felt at ease because the dog was at ease with him, and soon he began to go through the motions of getting used to the room. He sat on the hard chair by the wall; he stretched out on the bed; then he looked at himself in the dresser mirror; he walked slowly around the room and then invited Dan to sit on the bed with him.

"Not so bad, eh, Dan?" he asked, and the dog agreed with three impulsive thumps of his tail on the bed. "I think you're my friend," Luke said, and a remarkably intelligent expression shone in the dog's amber eye; his head twisted a little to one side; the right forepaw came reaching for Luke's hand. In the world there were some people who could talk to animals, Luke believed, and understand everything they said. Now he wondered if he were such a person. "Dan," he said, putting his head close to the dog's, "were you waiting and knowing I was coming? It's important, Dan. Tell me."

Lying with his head on his right forepaw and his one bright eye alert while Luke kept repeating, "Tell me, tell me, I'll understand," he suddenly lifted his head and gave an expectant eager little bark. At that moment the indolent and sleepy old dog was bright and alive and expectant.

"Sure, I get it, I get it," Luke said eagerly and he put his head down in the dog's warm soft flank. "We'll always understand each other," he whispered. "We'll know what goes on, won't we?"

Out over the lake the stars were coming out. The water was shining in the dusk. The evening breeze was rustling the window curtains. Sitting at the end of the bed from where he could look out over the lake and watch the moon rise, Luke began to feel lonely and he wondered about that dim world where his father was now. Wherever he was, could he be aware that his son was there at the window? His father had said, "I won't be far away, Luke." Now, of course, his father would be a spirit. But as a spirit he would have a power he had never had on the earth. There had been tales of men who encountered spirits and talked with them. If it were so, no spirit would be more anxious to talk with an earthly creature than his father would be to talk to him. But the time would have to be right, the place right, a place cool and silent, like a rendezvous in ancient time, a sacred rendezvous.

In the woods around the sawmill and on the lake water and even out on the island Indians had lived and died and Dr. Baldwin had often explained to Luke that in nature the Indians had found spirits everywhere. In the woods and on the rivers there would be places where these spirits could come close to those who sought them. As he pondered over these mysteries it was as if he himself were already making a plan. For an hour he sat in a dream. Then the cool air and the night breeze from the water suddenly made him feel sleepy. He got undressed slowly. The dog, watching, hesitated fearfully, then put his paw up on the bed. When Luke did not protest he jumped up on the bed and lay there all night.

4. The Hills
Were Really Blue

In the morning Uncle Henry asked Luke to go over to the mill with him and look around. As they left the house together the dog, who had been sleeping on the veranda, raised his head, came down from the veranda, and followed them diffidently for a few steps, his eye on Luke, waiting for an invitation to follow.

Luke knew that Dan was following him and when they got to the mill he remembered that Sam Carter had known the dog was not supposed to be there. To avoid trouble he turned. "Better run back to the house, Dan," he said. "I'll see you later."

"Is Dan following us into the mill?" Uncle Henry said. "That's funny. Dan hasn't done that for years. He knows he shouldn't be here."

"I guess he followed me, Uncle Henry."

"Go on, Dan. Get moving," Uncle Henry said impatiently. "Go on. Go back to the house and go to sleep again."

His good eye hopefully on Luke, the dog finally turned and ambled away, although he stopped once and turned to watch them.

"Dan's certainly a nice dog, Uncle Henry," Luke said quickly.

"Yeah. The poor old fellow certainly has no bad instincts," Uncle Henry agreed. "Of course, every dog has his day, and Dan has had his day. You see, Luke," he began, availing himself quickly of the opportunity to show Luke that there was sound sensible thinking behind his own idle observation, "Dan used to be good for hunting, but not now. I don't do any more hunting either. Of course, Dan used to be a good watchdog, but I have a hunch now he'd sleep through a fire. In fact, Luke, now that you call my attention to it..."

"I didn't call your attention to it, Uncle Henry."

"Eh. Well, no, Luke. But I mean if Dan's no good even as a watchdog and is half blind, well, it's just about time to get rid of him."

"But maybe Dan would like to be used for something."

"We still use him as a watchdog. Well, one of these days I'll have to get around to dealing with Dan," Uncle Henry said with a shrug.

His tone and his words had frightened Luke, who tried to tell himself that Uncle Henry had been so casual he was not really concerned about Dan. A little later on, Uncle

Henry might see how alive and eager the dog could be with him, Luke, and grow to admire him again.

In the mill Luke caught a whiff of the fine rich sweet smell of fresh wood, which was like an exotic perfume out of the depth of the forest. The workmen were all coming in, each one saying respectfully, "Good morning, Mr. Baldwin," with Uncle Henry answering crisply. "Good morning, Joe." "Good morning, Mr. Baldwin," "Good morning, Steven." "Good morning, Mr. Baldwin." "Good morning, Willie." Even Sam Carter said softly, "Good morning, Mr. Baldwin," and Uncle Henry answered cheerfully, "Morning Sam." Old Sam Carter's greeting seemed to come from way back in the depths of his being. It was a powerful effort at a show of grace. But his eyes were truly respectful.

Uncle Henry liked all his men to greet him cheerfully in the morning and they all knew it. If any man had greeted him with a sullen face, he would have resented it, his big neck would have reddened, he would have been disappointed, and he would have decided that such a workman was not completely happy in the mill and therefore his usefulness was impaired; he would have fired him quickly. No man who brooded could go on working for Uncle Henry.

The first thing Luke learned was that men who worked for Uncle Henry had an extraordinary respect for him and treated him as a very impressive man who was there to make up their minds for them because nothing that happened around the mill could truly baffle him.

The saws had started to whirl, and inside the mill the

shriek was a more frenzied sound than any Luke had ever heard. "You just look around, Luke. Get the picture in your mind," Uncle Henry said. "I'll explain all this another time"; and giving Luke a friendly slap on the back he went into the office.

As he wandered around, Luke knew he would love the sawmill; it was so fresh, clean and exciting. A great log was being ripped to pieces by the saws, and as he watched, the saws seemed to hypnotize him; it was the horror of imagining what would happen to him if he were ever caught on one of the logs and drawn toward the spinning saw. He could hardly turn away to watch the slow-moving belt on which were various kinds of wood. A man in blue overalls stood lifting off these pieces of wood, separating them as he recognized them by the grain and smell. Another belt, slow-moving like an escalator, drew up the heavy logs into the path of the saw. Luke hung around the mill until lunch time and then after lunch he and Uncle Henry drove into town to buy the things Luke needed for school. It was a bright sunny afternoon and on the way to town Luke watched the blue mountains rising beyond the town, for the road seemed to be running straight and true into those mountains which were as blue as the bay, and bluer, for the bay's blueness was broken with whitecaps raised by a wind from the north, these whitecaps running diagonally to the road and sparkling in the sun.

They passed the railroad tracks, the little bridge over the creek, and then over to the right was the station and behind the station the shipyard and the harbor. They passed a fine brick house with wide green lawns which was owned by J. C. Highbottom, the town's wealthiest man, who was a wholesale grocer, then the Catholic church, and then on to the wide, clean, brick-paved main street.

And then Luke began to learn something else about Uncle Henry. He was not stingy. It was not that he was exactly generous; he simply did not believe that in the long run it was profitable to be stingy. When they went into Alvin Slater's gents furnishing store, Alvin Slater knew Uncle Henry was not the kind of man who looked for bargains. Uncle Henry wanted a pair of shoes for Luke. "Show me something substantial, Alvin," he said. "Leather. Not paper. This boy will want to get around a little and I don't want him going around on his uppers."

After Mr. Slater had fitted a shoe on Luke and had asked him to walk up and down Uncle Henry kept repeating, "Is that a first-class shoe for a boy, Alvin? I want the most serviceable pair of shoes you've got. If they don't stand up, I'll be in here breathing down your neck."

Alvin Slater, who wore glasses and had a fine shiny bald head, was deeply concerned. "I recommend that shoe, Mr. Baldwin," he said pompously. "I know what you want and I stand behind that shoe. Now what else did you have in mind for the lad?"

"I want pants, heavy serviceable stuff, and a sweater or two, and a windbreaker." Turning to Luke he explained carefully, "Don't ever buy shoddy stuff, Luke. You might as well keep your money in your pocket. You've got to learn to recognize a real value. Never mind what it looks like at the first glance. Don't ever be taken in by appearances, my boy."

"I get the idea, Uncle Henry," Luke said importantly.

"Always remember that in the long run you pay for what you get. That's life. Anything of real value costs something in this world. You'll soon find out."

"Yeah, that's right, Uncle Henry."

"Will the lad try these breeks on, Mr. Baldwin?"

"Are they big enough to fit him next year?"

"I've allowed for that, Mr. Baldwin."

"Go into that back room and try them on, Luke, and you might as well leave them on, eh?"

They were a pair of brown corduroy breeks and they were too big, but when pulled up high above the waist they looked all right. Uncle Henry said they had a substantial quality.

Then walking along the sunlit street, walking in the shade, keeping in step with Uncle Henry, who was carrying the parcels, Luke felt proud; he understood that every storekeeper displayed his best merchandise when Uncle Henry came into his store.

"Now there's one other thing," Uncle Henry said with a little smile. "Come on, my boy."

On they went past the flour and feed store, the Josephson undertaking parlor, the bright new grocery store of J. C. Highbottom, a little dry goods store run by an old lady named Mary Coling, an ice cream parlor which was surprisingly large, and on to the bicycle store where Uncle Henry said with a grin, "Go on in, Luke."

The little, bald, spectacled proprietor shook hands effusively with Uncle Henry; but it was an embarrassing kind of politeness; it was as if the man were a little too eager to have Uncle Henry's good opinion of him.

In the shop were many secondhand bicycles, and some cheap new ones too. "I want a serviceable bicycle for the boy, Mr. Skidmore," Uncle Henry said. "One that will stand up. One you can guarantee. Luke, here, will have to ride that bike every day. A piece of junk would be a waste of money. I don't propose to waste my money, Mr. Skidmore."

Without any haggling he bought a fine expensive heavy bicycle and paid with money from his wallet. It was a handsome deerskin wallet. Into this wallet he tucked the written guarantee of the bicycle's serviceability. Then he told Luke to take the bicycle out to the street and ride up and down for a few minutes and try it out. And while Uncle Henry and the proprietor stood at the door in the late sunlight, blinking their eyes, Luke, in his new heavy brown corduroy breeks, circled slowly around the street with a new pride of ownership. But even while he was steering carefully and smiling happily, it struck him that Uncle Henry wasn't trying to be generous with him. The bicycle and the clothes were things that were needed. A thing that was needed had to be obtained. A thing that was no longer needed had to be tossed aside.

Uncle Henry had left the storekeeper and was sauntering

along the street, still watching Luke. At the corner he called, "How would you like to ride it home and get used to it, Luke?"

"Oh, that would be swell," Luke said, as he dismounted at the curb. "Thanks, Uncle Henry."

"I'm counting on you looking after that bike, Luke."

"I'll ride all over this town," he said enthusiastically. "Yeah, and for one thing, Uncle Henry," he went on, pointing along the road that cut through the town and ran for miles beyond to the blue mountains, "some day I'll ride up to those blue mountains."

"Why up there, Luke?"

"I like the look of them, Uncle Henry. I like knowing they're there."

"Oh," Uncle Henry said, looking puzzled, "and why do you like having them there, Luke?"

"I like blue mountains. Well, those mountains are very blue," he said with satisfaction. "It would be nice to get close to them, wouldn't it, Uncle Henry?" he asked.

"Yes, and the first thing you'll discover when you get close to them is that they're not blue," Uncle Henry said, chuckling a little.

"Well, they're blue from here, Uncle Henry."

"Yes. The fact is they're not blue, and you've got sense enough to know it, my boy."

"I don't know that they're not blue, Uncle Henry."

"It's an illusion, Luke. Simply an optical illusion."

"Don't you like them for being so blue, Uncle Henry?"

"But the fact is they're not blue, Luke. It's a nice colorful effect, of course, which comes from sunlight and shadow and distance. The fact is that up there it's all farm land and woods and valleys just as it is down here." Then he chuckled again. "Luke, what would you say about a man who went on believing all his life those mountains were really blue? Would you say he was an idiot?"

"No."

"Why not?"

"Well, look at them, Uncle Henry."

"I don't care what they look like," Uncle Henry said irritably. "I've just told you."

"But they're blue, aren't they?"

"But the fact is, the fact, Luke..." Uncle Henry began patiently. With a sigh he shrugged and looked at Luke with a dubious expression. "You're a wee bit stubborn, Luke. Never mind. You follow me home." And he walked along the street to his car.

And following the car down the road through the town Luke, still imagining he was arguing with his uncle, kept repeating doggedly, "If a man painted those hills, he'd have to paint what he saw, wouldn't he?" "And if he didn't paint them blue it would be a lie. Because there they are—wonderfully blue, so what are you talking about?"

5. The Sacred Grove

O N the way to school Luke had company, for Dan automatically trotted behind the bicycle, and Luke grinning to himself, let the dog follow him for a quarter of a mile down the main road. What was so splendid about it was that he hadn't even whistled to Dan; he hadn't even looked back; he pedaled along slowly, grinning happily, knowing Dan was trailing him.

Of course, he couldn't let the dog follow him all the way to school. When they came to the big elm he got off the bike. "Dan, old boy," he said, "I leave you here. Don't worry, I'll be back about four o'clock. You hang around. Now stay here or go back. Go on, Dan."

No one could know how much he was getting to like that old dog. He liked the way Dan would lie down, flopping heavily, like a chair falling over. He liked the way he stretched, pushing out his forepaw, then leaning all his weight well back, then coming up slowly. And the way he came when called, the head down, the tail wagging, his body in a mincing motion as if he had the shakes.

When he had pedaled on about a hundred feet he looked around and Dan was standing in the middle of the road.

But the day at school did not go very well; Luke was a stranger, a kid from the city, a new kid; at noontime and at recess he stood around by himself looking self-possessed and aloof, to guard his shyness and to give the air of being contented and indifferent while waiting warily for someone to make friendly gestures. Some of the kids said, "Aw, he's a city kid, and look how stuck-up he is," because Luke, thinking of himself as a boy who was very wise about people and knew how to handle them, believed that if he appeared aloof and indifferent they would all be anxious to be friendly.

At three-thirty when they all rushed out of school and broke up into groups he rushed out too, but there was no group for him to join. While he was standing on the steps feeling lonely, Elmer Highbottom, who was two inches taller, lurched against him and cried, "Get out of the way, kid, or do you want something?" But when Luke raised his fists and awaited grimly, Elmer, seeing that Luke would fight, laughed derisively and left him alone. Luke sauntered toward his bicycle, wanting suddenly to get back to the mill.

On the road he found himself thinking again of the days when his father had hunted in the woods across the river from the mill. Even now, pedaling down the road, was it possible, he wondered, that his father could be watching him?

He was coming to the place by the side of the road where he had left Dan in the morning and when he made the little turn there was Dan lying down in the shade of an elm tree. "Hi, Dan," he yelled eagerly. Stretching, then shaking himself thoroughly, Dan came trotting out to the road to greet him.

Three times during the day the dog had returned to the spot. At noontime when he had been sleeping on the veranda he had suddenly stirred, wondering and testing the force of his instinct to go, and then he had trotted down to the road and had waited, moving around doubtfully. The dog was uneasy about not being able to pick out the right time. Returning to the house he had slept again. Two hours later he had looked up quickly as if feeling a curious prompting; then he had gone trotting quietly back to the elm tree.

"Say, Dan, I think you were asleep there. How did you know it was me coming down the road?" Luke asked. But the dog only circled cheerfully around the bike. He seemed to understand Luke's surprise and pleasure.

From that time on the dog would go that far along the road with him in the morning, and he would be there at that hour each day when he came home.

At the house after Luke had let his aunt know he was home, he came out and stood on the river bank looking across the river at the woods. He turned away, then turned again slowly. Frowning, he wondered why he could not go away.

Tied up at the bank was Uncle Henry's old rowboat and as he walked toward it he called, "Come on, Dan."

He did not row very well; his oars dipped too deeply into the water or slipped out without cutting the water and he hoped Uncle Henry could not see him. If Uncle Henry was watching, he would be sure to notice whether Luke was feathering the oars properly; he might even call out and insist on giving him a rowing lesson. So he avoided looking in the direction of the mill; he kept looking toward the woods.

Somewhere in the woods, in some cool grove where there was only a slant of sunlight, or maybe on a spot by the side of the river which would be secret and silent, he expected to draw close to his father. The fact that his father was dead still didn't have much meaning for him. Each morning he half expected to see him.

Letting the oars trail in the water he took the dog's head in his arms and explained solemnly, "You know what I'm thinking, Dan? Maybe you have ways of knowing and seeing and hearing that I haven't got. You know what I mean? If you can hear things I can't hear, then I guess you can see things I can't see. Isn't that right, Dan?" Licking Luke's hands, the dog expressed approval of the sound of his voice, the intimate tone, anything he might say.

Having crossed the river and pulled the boat up on the bank they headed upstream. It was as if Luke were looking for a path into the woods, believing that if there were such a path, his father, too, would have found the path and followed it. But instead of a path they found the brush becoming more tangled, primeval. A ledge of great jagged rocks made Luke feel that the region was ancient, his footstep was alien. While he was watching and hesitating, the impatient dog darted into the woods; then Luke followed eagerly.

Old fallen branches blocked the way, the ground was soft from rotting roots, tangled vines hung from the trees like the arms of an octopus, and the spruces and the hemlock so close together shut out the sunlight. "Keep going, Dan," he called encouragingly. But even the crack of a twig underfoot startled him as he followed and he kept looking around, always looking around slowly with the strange, lonely longing in his heart, wondering and expectant.

It was like going into the shadowed vaulted world of ghosts; in his imagination each stone and tree had its spirit; some of them good, some of them evil and determined to thwart him. When low underbrush or thorny twisting vines caught at his pant legs he slashed at them savagely with his stick, as if he suddenly believed that powerful demons could take the form of curling vines and twine around him and force him back. When he slashed at the vines the dog barked savagely.

Still there was no path. A big brown bird swooping low scared him and he ducked, but it was only a partridge; the wings seemed to him to be ten feet wide. In a little while he felt lost in the woods, only he knew that he could not be lost while Dan was there.

They came to a strange pool with floating gray, dead logs, and weeds gray too, and the underbrush around the pool gray and dead; a burned-out place with charred stumps and logs rotten with age. Luke's foot crunched the rotting logs into a brown dust. There was one mossy pool and then low swampland, and while he was looking over the swamp and dreading its evil smell and vast stagnation he heard a rustling near his foot. A fat brown snake four feet long glided toward another log. "Dan!" he yelled, terrified. The dog, leaping toward him, stiffened, the fur on his head and neck suddenly like bristles, his back arching, his one good eye on the eyes of the snake which did not retreat but spiraled a little and watched with malevolent calmness. Though barking furiously, Dan did not attack.

"Look out, Dan. Look out," Luke whispered. He wanted to run, but as he watched the tan markings and the black blotches on the snake's head he knew he should not run nor be driven back by this guardian of these dark regions. Retreating a little, his knees weak, he picked up a large flat rock and heaved it at the snake's head. The rock crunched against the curving body a foot behind the head and the snake, lashing out in a whirling motion, glided away and disappeared behind another fallen tree.

"Wow, was I scared, Dan!" Luke said. But Dan now did not look scared.

"You don't know what that snake really might be," Luke went on. "It was there like an evil monster, wasn't it, Dan?"

Circling around the swampy ground they headed for the slope where the trees thinned out, and where there was spruce and hemlock and sunlight.

Then suddenly the whole earth shook, and because he believed he was wandering in a shadowy world he was scared, his heart started to pound; he looked up and the branches and the leaves of the trees were all interlaced in a cloud of smoke that came drifting down darkly. As the smoke drifted by, a shaft of sunlight fell upon his wondering face, and he heard the lonely whistle of a train passing on the tracks which were on a ridge running through the woods. "Oh! It was only a train, Dan," he said with a sigh of relief.

Still looking around expectantly and reaching out for some little sound or sign or shadow or whisper that would be like a sudden familiar consolation, he seemed like a watchful boy going slowly through the woods looking for someone. They came to a little gully where there were second-growth pines and oaks, magnificent tall trees towering in the long slanting bars of sunlight with the air sweet and cool. Suddenly this place was like a haven of dignity and peace which they had come to after a difficult journey through dark evil swampy regions.

In this clearing was a huge rounded rock of quartz and gneiss, eight feet high and flattened at the top. Around it were smaller rocks jutting out of the grass. But this great rock was set down there among the trees like a huge flattened ball. Walking around the rock Luke looked at it and pondered and wondered if he could climb to the top. On the mossy sloping sides were rounded holes, and little ledges. He began to haul himself up.

When he was halfway to the top Dan began to bark, so he called, "Come on, Dan." The dog leaped up after him, but he began to slide and Luke grabbed him by the forepaws; then Dan became like a worm, his body flattening out against the surface as he came crawling up to the top. There they sat down together.

As Luke sat with his arms folded around his knees looking at the tops of the trees rising around him in the sunlight, he suddenly realized how lonely he had been since he had come to the sawmill. "Where am I?" he thought, and looking all around he asked, "What am I doing here?"

But no soft voice answered and broke his loneliness. No matter how closely he listened or how long he waited, he heard no sound.

But Dan, who had been resting with his head on his paws, his pink tongue hanging out as he breathed jerkily, rose slowly; the fur on his neck stiffened; his ears were up and he growled a little; it was like a low threatening alert rumble. Dan's head swung around slowly.

"What is it, Dan?" Luke asked anxiously.

Dan now was watching quietly, offering no threat, watching instead with great but friendly curiosity. Suddenly he barked three times.

"Dan! Dan, what is it?" Luke pleaded in a worried tone. "What are you barking at, Dan? I don't see anything"—but now he was frightened by the mysterious presence that Dan could feel, but which he himself could not see. With his hands clenched, his head raised and his eyes fearful, he turned slowly and looked all around. The back of his neck twitched; it was as if he were being watched, only he saw now that the dog was not scared and it reassured him. The silence became friendly. Then Dan slowly turned his head, the one good eye on Luke as if asking him, "Is it all right? I'm not worried if you're not."

Longing as he did to believe that his father was not far away and could come close to him, Luke was awed. The dog seemed to have the strange power to see and feel an unseen presence. In Luke's thoughts there was only one unseen presence, and so he was comforted and yet shaken. Kneeling with his arms around Dan, he whispered, "Oh, Dan, I wish I could see and feel things as you do." In acknowledgment of this tribute, the dog licked Luke's hand.

For a long time they sat there at peace with each other and content. All Luke's thoughts were of his father, and half dreaming he found himself explaining how strange he found the life around the sawmill.

They stayed there until Dan stood up and looked down the slope of the rock and started to feel his way down as if he were implying there was no use staying there any longer.

Before trotting off through the woods, Luke looked for a time at the rock. "We'll come here, Dan. We'll often come here," he whispered. It was like the sharing of a mysterious secret and the beginning of a building up of a secret world that nobody at the sawmill could know anything about.

They made their way downstream to the boat, and when they were in the boat, with the mill and the house there in the sunlight, he knew that he must never let Uncle Henry know what had happened in the woods, for what had happened belonged to that world of strange wonders that Uncle Henry despised, and therefore it belonged in the secret life he could share only with Dan.

6. Nobody Fools Uncle Henry

LUKE seemed to his Aunt Helen to be a practical useful boy to have around the house, for he put the screens on the front windows for her, mended two of them, and appreciated how important it was to her to keep flies out of the house. She offered to give him five cents for every ten flies he killed, and one afternoon he was working industriously with the fly swatter. He knew, however, that he wasn't going to get rich killing flies so early in the season.

When he was in the kitchen, concentrating on one stubborn fly that would not abandon its secure position on the ceiling, he heard his aunt talking to a man at the front door. When the man's voice faded away and Aunt Helen came back to the kitchen, Luke went out to the veranda.

Standing beside his car was a man of sixty-five in clean blue overalls, who had a leathery, lined face, a straggling

moustache, and wise, steady gray eyes. When Luke got a
little closer to this man the lines on his face seemed to have
come from years of smiling. His name was Alex Kemp and
he lived in the red brick house along the road a piece from
the sawmill. He had a herd of cows and had come to
deliver milk.

The collie, who had been asleep on the veranda, got up
and waddled over to Luke, who knelt down to stroke his
head as he watched Mr. Kemp.

"Ah, you're the boy I've heard about," Mr. Kemp called.
"Didn't take you long to make a friend of Dan, did it?
Come here, Dan."

Wagging his tail slowly and shaking his body, the old dog
went down the steps to old Mr. Kemp, who rubbed the
collie as if he had known him a long time. Seeing that Dan
liked the old man, Luke also approached him and Mr.
Kemp sat down on the running board of the car.

Some men, old or middle-aged, have a way of being at
ease with a boy at once by not trying to be too friendly with
him, but simply by letting everything come easily and naturally and taking it for granted they are not separated by
the difference in age.

"Warm day, eh, son?" Mr. Kemp said, mopping his forehead. "That's a nice dog you've got there. Dan and I are old
friends. I can remember when Dan was a pup. Best-looking
dog around here then. Say, son, why don't you get an old
comb and comb out that loose hair on him?"

"What'll that do with him?" Luke asked guardedly.

"Make him look like a new dog. Smarten him up."

"He's pretty smart the way he is," Luke said quickly, but he was looking closely at Dan and observing that around the dog's neck there was hair that looked dead and matted. The glossy sheen that ought to have been a fine old collie's distinction was lacking. And suddenly he began to feel elated. "Maybe a little combing and fixing might make Dan look younger, would it, Mr. Kemp?"

"Ever see a lady fresh from a beauty parlor?"

"No, I guess I haven't."

"The point is they also feel young, Luke."

"Yeah, that's important, isn't it, Mr. Kemp? I mean for a lady, and maybe for a dog too."

"Try it with Dan and you'll find he'll go right along with you."

"I'll go to work on him, Mr. Kemp."

"Sure, and why don't you and Dan come up some night and help me bring the cows home?"

"Okay, Mr. Kemp."

"It's a deal then, son," Mr. Kemp said as he got into the car and waved, his eyes still gentle and twinkling with sympathetic amusement.

And Luke stood for a moment watching the old car going down the road as if something about the old man puzzled him; then he turned and hurried into the house and into the kitchen where his Aunt Helen was baking, her plump face pink and shining from the heat, and he asked her if she would give him an old comb and brush. She made many clucking noises mixed with tolerant sighs when he explained why he wanted the brush; but she was willing to indulge him a little and when she had taken her pies out of the oven she got a brush and a comb.

Whistling for Dan he found a cool spot in the shade of the pile of cordwood at the back of the house, sat down and began to comb the lose hair from under the dog's neck.

In his mind there was a picture of the surprise which would show on Uncle Henry's face when he saw how sprightlier and younger Dan looked, and he longed to hear him say, "Why, whatever made me think Dan was an old dog not much good for anything? He looks as good as he ever did, Luke." The dead hair came out in little tufts. He combed and tugged at the old matted hair. Some of it was like cotton batten and he could lift it out with his fingers. No matter how vigorously he combed, Dan did not complain.

For the collie this careful combing was like an old memory of a care and concern for his appearance he hadn't felt in anybody for a long time; he took it as a gesture of affection. In each tug of the comb Dan felt the beginning of a restoration of a lost importance.

It took Luke an hour and a half to comb out the loose hair, which was there in a pile big enough to stuff a sofa pillow. When he had finished the combing he began to brush Dan; he liked brushing him; each stroke of the brush brought a shine to the coat, and soon he had brushed out the little white apron which is part of a collie's distinction.

"I don't do it very well, Dan," Luke apologized, "but you certainly look like a different dog to me. Anybody could see now you're a thoroughbred. Walk up and down there, Dan. Go on, boy."

The collie put his forepaws out stiffly, his head came down, he drew all his weight back as he always did when stretching, then moved around in a little circle, waiting with his good eye glowing, his tail wagging expectantly.

The collie now wanted to prance and play a little. He swung away from Luke and scurried around the yard, his nose to the ground as if chasing a rat until he found a stick about a foot long; snapping it up, the collie returned to Luke and dropped the stick at his feet; he nodded an invitation to the play and backed away encouragingly as if giving Luke a chance to grab the stick. They both grabbed at it together, Dan tugging one way, Luke the other, with Dan growling and worrying and deliberately yielding a little ground. It really wasn't hard to get the stick away from the collie, whose grip was no longer fierce and strong because of the bad teeth. So Luke humored him a little; he let Dan tear the stick from his hand. Laughing happily he watched Dan do a little victory march which was a kind of strut as he pranced in a circle, shaking the stick in the air.

The shadows on that side of the house had lengthened. The mill saws were suddenly still ... voices carried from the mill. Two of the workmen with their lunch pails went down the road. From the porch came the sound of Uncle Henry's heavy step. Then Luke called out eagerly, "Could you come here a minute, Uncle Henry?"

Uncle Henry came around the side of the house with his brisk, busy, long stride, mopping his sunburned forehead with a big white very clean handkerchief, and he smiled when he saw Luke squatting beside the pile of dog hair, the brush still in his hand.

"What do you think of Dan now, Uncle Henry?" Luke asked eagerly.

"Been pretty busy, eh, Luke? What are you going to do with all that hair? Stuff a mattress?" Uncle Henry asked.

"Dan looks pretty spry. Just like a young dog...almost, doesn't he, Uncle Henry?" Luke encouraged him. "That's the way he should look. That's the way he really feels, Uncle Henry."

"Well, there's less chance of his getting eczema with that old hair combed out," Uncle Henry agreed. "But he's still blind in one eye, Luke, and he's still got a bad leg."

Looming up over Luke and Dan, his arms folded across his chest, Uncle Henry eyed them both quizzically. As was natural and inevitable with him, he decided to draw out of the occasion a useful moral that might be of value to a growing boy.

"Yes," he said, with a little chuckle, "a man who didn't look closely and took dogs and men at their face value might be deceived a little by that primping you've done, Luke. But with dogs and men in this world it's often all a big front. A man and his work will often stand up under a quick glance, but once you look closely—once you know what you're looking for, you see to it that you get your value for your money. Take Dan there, a man should disregard all that brushing. Take his mouth, see. Come here, Dan. Look at the teeth, Luke. Look at the eyes. See what I mean? In half a minute you know Dan's a washed-up old dog. That primping shouldn't take anybody in. Always try and see things for what they are, my boy. Even when you're dealing only with yourself, face the real facts if you want to get on in the world."

Smiling, and yet serious, he stood there, his legs wide apart, looming up over them, ready to answer questions, but the questions didn't come from Luke, who was too distressed. Nor did Dan wag his tail. Uncle Henry could be a maddening man. "Well, come on in and get washed up for dinner, Luke," Uncle Henry said cheerfully.

And Luke whispered to Dan, "He's got his mind made up, Dan. That's all. But if he can't see that you look like a million dollars, then he's the one who's blind in one eye—not you."

7. Another Kind of Wise Man

THEY would sit down at the table with the screened windows wide open and a cool breeze blowing from the lake. At that time of year, the end of May, it was chilly when the sun went down, but Uncle Henry couldn't get enough fresh air. There was no use complaining of the draft from the window. Aunt Helen was convinced that no one got a cold from a draft or from feeling cold; one got a cold only from a germ. These positive opinions embarrassed Luke, who couldn't get used to them. It was not like home. And on the table the knives and forks and spoons were not set down as his father's housekeeper would have done it. Big bowls of food were put down on the table. And the smell of the house was different; it was a fine clean smell, but it had not yet become the smell of his own house, or he would not still be noticing it.

"What's on your mind, son?" Uncle Henry asked suddenly.

"A penny for your thoughts, Luke," Aunt Helen said.

"I wasn't really thinking anything."

"Oh, come on, son, you were in a dream."

"I was wondering about that Mr. Kemp. He's a queer man, isn't he?"

"What's queer about him, Luke?"

"I don't know; he's just queer—different."

"Maybe he's queer, Luke," Uncle Henry said, "but a pretty shrewd fellow. In some ways I've a lot of respect for Mr. Kemp. Mind you, I don't agree with him about many things, Luke, but he's a good neighbor, and an intelligent man. I have a lot of respect for him."

"Isn't he just a farmer, like other farmers around here?"

"Why, yes, and he has those cows. Look here, Luke. You tell me why you think he's queer." Turning to his wife he added, "A boy often has a shrewd insight into people. I'm interested in what Luke sees in Mr. Kemp. Maybe the boy has real insight."

"Oh, I wasn't thinking anything important, Uncle Henry," Luke said quickly.

"I know. I know. But what do you make of Mr. Kemp? What did you notice about him?"

"Well, he certainly seems able to take his time. I noticed the way he takes his time—for one thing."

"That's true. Yes, Luke, go on."

"And he sort of lazes around—as if he never got excited. Does he ever get excited, Uncle Henry?"

"I don't think he does, Luke. Come to think of it."

"I don't mean he's lazy, Uncle Henry."

"Oh, I know what you mean. He's certainly not lazy."

"It's as if—well, as if he's sort of smiling to himself inside."

"A philosopher," Aunt Helen said brightly.

"Is that what he is, Aunt Helen? What's a philosopher?"

"Oh, he's just a nice old man, Luke. I suppose that's what a philosopher is—a nice old man."

"Let Luke go on, Helen."

"I'm not stopping him, Henry."

"I liked him. It was just a feeling I had," Luke said deprecatingly, for Uncle Henry was nodding seriously. Luke couldn't imagine that anything he had to say about people would be truly illuminating to such a shrewd man as Uncle Henry. "I guess I mean," he blurted out, "that Mr. Kemp seems to have been looking at places and things a long time and maybe he knows what's important and what's not important."

"No. No. No, Luke," Uncle Henry protested vigorously. "There you go wrong. There I disagree with you. Although, mind you, my boy, you've been very shrewd about Mr. Kemp. You have eyes in your head, Luke. The making of a man of good judgment. It's all a man needs. You can't get anywhere in the world unless you can appraise people at their proper value."

Reaching over, he patted Luke's shoulder approvingly. "Very good, my boy." Clearing his throat like a chairman taking charge of a meeting to sum up and make the whole matter clear, he went on, "It's true Mr. Kemp has been looking at places and things a long time, Luke. But at the one place, the one sky, the one lake, his own wood lot—for fifty years. Why, Luke, old Mr. Kemp has a university education. His father, you know, left him some money, and what did he do? Why he's come back to this place and he sits up there growing old with his land and just taking his time. Ah, it's a regrettable thing, Luke, when an intelligent, educated man like Mr. Kemp doesn't try to do anything with the world. No feeling for action at all. And you're wrong in thinking he knows what's important. I don't think he knows what's important. He doesn't at all. That man has got things all twisted. But it puzzles me. It's hard to explain. If he only applied himself to functioning usefully, he would see things differently, and he wouldn't puzzle me."

"But, Henry, he has the best dairy cows around here. You must admit that," Aunt Helen said.

"Oh, yes, yes, but he simply indulges himself with those cows."

"Well, he asked me to come up with Dan and bring the cows in with him," Luke said. "What do you think?"

"Why, go ahead, Luke."

"I think I'll go up tonight," Luke said.

Going up the road later on with Dan, Luke wasn't quite sure why he wanted to get the cows with old Mr. Kemp. The desire to be with someone who seemed to share his appreciation of Dan, which was the real reason, was not clear to him and he imagined that he was only seeking a little fun doing something he had never done before.

It was about seventy-thirty and the sun was like a big red ball rolling across the tips of the trees to the west. Up the road, far beyond the end of the road and over the town, the blue mountains gleamed with patches of yellow light and then the hills suddenly becoming a deeper blue took on a purple tinge. On the road, which was made of pounded gravel, were small jutting rocks, and Dan walked delicately at the side of the road in the grass where the walking was easier on the paws. When they came to Mr. Kemp's house Luke hesitated shyly, looking at the tall three-storied brick structure with the small veranda. If Mr. Kemp had been sitting on the veranda reading the paper, everything would have been easy, but he wasn't there.

"Maybe we won't go in, eh, Dan?" he asked as Dan looked up at him expectantly. "Maybe we'll just go on for a walk by ourselves." But Dan, now going lazily up the path as if on familiar ground, turned to wait for him. If he had ready a few noncommittal, nonchalant remarks to make as soon as he saw Mr. Kemp, Luke thought, he might justify his presence there. He could say, "Dan turned in here, Mr. Kemp, so I thought I might as well come in, too." If Mr. Kemp were busy he could say, "Come on, Dan, we've got to get on our way."

With a self-conscious swagger he loafed up the path kicking idly at little stones and sticks as he listened apprehensively. He went on to the back of the house and from there he could see the cow sheds which didn't look like battered old sheds; they were splendidly clean and painted white; a hired man in a blue shirt was raking up the ground in front of one of the sheds. As this hired man looked up, and Luke prepared to withdraw, Mr. Kemp came out of the back door. He was wearing a windbreaker and a straw hat. "Hello, there, Luke," he called, waving his hand enthusiastically. "I was wondering when you'd show up," and he snapped his fingers at Dan, who trotted to him.

"I was out for a walk and Dan turned in here," Luke began solemnly. "I thought I'd come in, Mr. Kemp."

"Why, you wouldn't be much of a neighbor if you didn't come in, Luke. Why, you certainly did a good job on Dan. He looks about ten pounds thinner, a fine, sleek dog."

"He looks younger, don't you think, Mr. Kemp?"

"Years younger, Luke."

"Uncle Henry didn't think so."

"Maybe your uncle didn't really look at him."

"Oh, he looked at him, all right."

"But not as if he had never seen him before."

"Yeah. That's right, and that's important, eh, Mr. Kemp?"

"It certainly is important, Luke. Come on, let's get those cows."

"Well, what do we do, Mr. Kemp?" Luke asked enthusiastically.

"I'll tell you what I do, Luke," Mr. Kemp said amiably as they passed the stable and headed for the open pasture land stretching out from the back of the house. "I just get behind the last cow in the field and say, 'Co boss,' and throw a little pebble at her heels and she lurches along like a drunken sailor, and soon they all start moving. There are only about twelve of them. But an energetic lad like you with a smart dog might round them up like a cowboy riding the range. See what I mean?"

Turning to the left, they cut by the corner of the Kemp wood lot and ahead was the pasture land stretching out, rolling a little, in the rising mist. From there you could see the grazing cows, fat brown-and-white Jersey cows. "I'll tell you what," Mr. Kemp said, when they came to a smooth flat stone. "I'm a lazy man. I could sit here and smoke a pipe and watch you and Dan handle the job, Luke. You might have the making of a great cowboy. How do I know? Don't be afraid of making a little noise and if you want to you can ride herd on them. Let's see how you can handle this, son."

With a happy grin on his face he set down and fumbled in his pocket for his pipe. What pleased Luke was that he could see that Mr. Kemp enjoyed being there with him and would also enjoy watching him round up the cows. In the little silence between them their eyes met, and Luke had the strange feeling that Mr. Kemp knew all that he, Luke, would like to do, and that these things were right and good because they had been done many times before; the contemplation of these things seemed to give Mr. Kemp a simple pleasure in being alive in the world. Of course, Luke didn't express it to himself in this way. But he had a sudden friendly awareness that everything, simply everything, the time of the evening, the cows in the field, the sun going down, himself there with the dog, was all as it should be. Grinning, he said, "I think I can get them heading this way, Mr. Kemp."

"Take it easy, son. Once they pass this stone they're on their way, and Joe, my hired man, will get them in the sheds."

"Come on, Dan," Luke called, and they both began to trot across the pasture. Before they had gone fifty paces he felt himself imbued with a strange excitement, stimulating his imagination and giving a fantastic glow to the whole scene. The mist from the lush pasture land rose around him like the low thin smoke from campfires; hovering over the ground it swirled like smoke settling after artillery fire. The cows became a great herd that had to be rounded up quickly and driven along the pass in the direct fire of the rustlers who were there in the campfire smoke. His regular trot became a gallop. As Dan galloped with him and he called softly, "Will we ride 'em, Dan! Give the word, Dan. Of course, there's only you and me." He addressed Dan as the leader, as if he recognized that Dan, from then on in their play and in his dreams, was to be the one who was older and possessed of an ancient, instinctive wisdom.

When they were far across the field beyond the last lazy brown cow Luke, suddenly swerved as if reining in his mount, a mount that only he could ride, and Dan swerved too. Luke didn't deign to pick up a stone or stick and hurl it at the lazy cow grazing there peacefully. He yelled, "Just as you say, Dan. Hi, hi, to the hills. To the hills. Sure, we'll ride 'em, Dan," and he rushed at the cows. Dan, now barking fiercely, darted at the legs of the startled cow, which jerked up its head, backed away, lashing its flanks with its tail, and trotted heavily away from the boy and the dog.

Forgetting about his lame leg the collie swerved around crazily with Luke, hurling himself at the rear hoofs and cutting in recklessly under the belly. Each time Luke yelled, "Hi, hi, hi," the old dog barked with fierce excitement. But the mist was rising, the mist like a terrible barrage smoke from the hidden gunfire, coming closer. While Dan circled and barked and drove the herd together, Luke was left alone to face the rustlers. Panting, he dropped to his knees as if the horse, perfectly trained, was kneeling beside him; he took aim; he heard the roar of his gun. But that little twinge in his shoulder—a hot stab—yes—he had been hit, the shoulder suddenly became painful. He let his left arm fall heavily at his side. But he couldn't abandon the position, not when Dan counted on him; not when Dan, riding as he never rode before and firing in the air, had three of the herd trotting along in the beginning of the stampede. "Good old Dan, he can do the job alone if they don't wing him," Luke whispered to his horse. "Come on, boy, on your feet." Mounting, he rode after Dan, ducking low on the saddle.

"Hi, hi, Dan," he yelled. And Dan trotted back to him, panting and blowing and limping badly now. "I'm sorry, Dan. Maybe I let you down. But they got me in the shoulder. Oh, Dan, they got you in the leg." Dan's good eye only danced and shone with pleasure. From one of the cows came a long "Moo-oo," and then an answering "Moo-oo," from across the field.

"They're all in motion now, Dan. It's just as you figured it. Soon we'll be out of danger. I'll try and hold out, Dan. Soon the whole great herd will be in motion. And woe betide those rustlers if they try to stop them. They'll be trampled underfoot, pounded to a pulp. Don't worry about me, Dan, I'm taking it easy."

As they rode off again across the field, he saw with concern that Dan, limping badly, wasn't swerving and barking. Though tiring, he wanted to go on. With his good eye he said he wanted to go on. So Luke, too, began to limp badly. "Oh, oh," he moaned. "They got me in the leg, too, Dan. I'm afraid I'm holding you back."

His moan was so real that Dan, wheeling, looked up with the same intelligent and sympathetic concern that Luke had offered to him; the dog tried to jump up and put his paws on Luke's chest; the tongue came out, reaching for Luke's hands. "I can hold out if you can, Dan," Luke cried. And they whirled on after the cows.

Driven by the shouting, circling and barking, the twelve cows now in a group moved slowly in the direction of the corner of the wood lot and the lane leading to the sheds. No longer could they be startled into trotting, they loafed along, mooing and swinging their heads at the barking dog. But they were like a real herd with their lashing tails, their big surprised eyes and their snorting nostrils. And to Luke their animal smell was like a strange intoxicating odor, belonging to his dream in which he rode along, lean and tired on his saddle now, chatting with his boss, Dan, for the herd was filing past the outpost, where Mr. Kemp waited.

"Well, Luke," Mr. Kemp called, "that was a great show."

"Eh? Was it?" Luke answered with an embarrassed smile, for in his mind he was still far away from Mr. Kemp; but now, coming closer to him in his thoughts, and then suddenly very close to him, he smiled shyly.

"Where's Dan?" he asked awkwardly. "Hey, Dan, come here. Here we are back with Mr. Kemp." He seemed to be apologizing to Dan for restoring him to the reality of the pasture land, and Mr. Kemp, and the sawmill, and making him an old dog again. But Dan was now willing to be quiet. He flopped down at Luke's feet. "Was it all right the way we did it, Mr. Kemp?" Luke asked.

"It was never done better, Luke."

"Well, that's fine."

"Yes, Luke, it was done with dash and distinction and splendid imagination."

"Dan's a little lame. I hope his leg won't get worse, Mr. Kemp. I hope it doesn't stiffen up. I don't think he's such a very old dog, do you, Mr. Kemp?"

"Oh, Dan's good for a few years yet, Luke."

"If you owned him you wouldn't want to get rid of him, would you, Mr. Kemp?"

"Me? Well, not if he meant much to me, Luke. A man never deliberately gets rid of anything he loves, Luke, does he? But the trouble is, a dog often has more loyalty than a man and sometimes he can't count on his owner's loyalty. Come on, sit down and rest awhile, Luke."

As Luke sat down Mr. Kemp said rhetorically, "Let's sit upon the ground awhile and tell sad stories of the death of kings. That's a quotation from 'Richard the Second,' son, a play. In our case, it's the death of dogs we're talking about."

He began to tell a story about a dog he had owned when he was a boy, a dog which had grown up with him. He talked in a slow, drawling tone. It was getting a little cooler and the night breeze that follows the sinking sun was rustling through the leaves of the trees. Luke, sitting beside the eloquent old man, had his face raised to him, his eyes wondering.

"And this dog, a little Boston bull, was pretty old," Mr. Kemp went on. "I don't know how old, maybe twelve years. It was going along the road with me one day, trotting on ahead, and suddenly it seemed to stiffen and roll over. Well, it was a heart attack. Now here's the funny thing, son. That dog knew it was finished. Yet it kept trying to twist its body around in a pathetic convulsive movement so it could turn its head to me and look at me, look right into my eyes. It wanted to make this last gesture of affectionate loyalty as it died on the road."

"I guess that dog liked you, Mr. Kemp. It must have liked you a lot."

"Of course, I liked the dog, too."

After a long pause, Luke said suddenly. "My father died of a heart attack, Mr. Kemp."

"Is that a fact. I'm sorry, son. I didn't know."

"That's all right, Mr. Kemp. But what you just said about that dog is, well…it's an important story," Luke said solemnly.

"Yes, it is, Luke. In some ways a dog has a much superior instinct to a man. And mind you, a spiritual instinct, Luke. They say dogs have no souls, don't they? Well, how they know is beyond me. Of course, the plain truth is, they don't know. The plain fact is that a dog's sense of love and loyalty and devotion is often greater than that of its owner."

They had got up and were going slowly along the path, the smoke from Mr. Kemp's pipe rising in blue wisps, and they were talking as one man to another, pondering over the inexplicable mysteries of human conduct.

"Now take a fellow I knew who had a cottage way down the lake there. Name of Brown. Your Uncle Henry knew him well, Luke. This man lived alone with his dog, a collie with a little husky in it, and they were inseparable companions. Used to see them everywhere and that fellow claimed he was never lonely when his dog was around. Now you'd think, wouldn't you, Luke, that that fellow would be heartbroken if anything happened to his friend. Well, as the dog grew old we used to say, 'Poor old Brown, what'll he do when that dog goes?' Then one day the dog died and I happened to be down that way and I saw old Brown dragging it into the woods to bury it. And then what? Well, two days later Brown had another dog. That was all there was to it. I asked him if he didn't miss his old pet and he said the new dog was just as good, and served exactly the same purpose. All our sympathy for Brown's broken heart was wasted. See what I mean, Luke?"

"Yes," Luke said profoundly. "I guess that man was what you call practical. Is that right?"

"He certainly was practical."

"My Uncle Henry is a practical man, too."

"Is that a fact?" Mr. Kemp said, smiling to himself.

"Yes, he's the most practical man I know."

At the stables, Joe the hired man had driven the cows into the stalls; they could see him sitting on a stool in one of the stalls, a pail under the swollen udder, and he was squeezing the teats expertly. A stream of warm milk spurted in the pail. The whitewashed stalls were very clean, and there was the smell of warm milk, cows and manure mixed with the smell of the bush and the fields in the twilight. Luke seemed to be watching intently the hired man's expert manipulation of the milk-squirting teats, but in his own mind he could see Uncle Henry dragging a dog along the beach just as Mr. Kemp's friend Brown had done it, and on his uncle's face was the same unconcerned expression.

"You know, Mr. Kemp," Luke began cautiously, "old Dan there is really a remarkable animal."

"Is that a fact, Luke?"

"Yeah, Dan knows things," Luke said slowly. He longed to explain what had happened in the woods; to say, "Dan knew I was wondering if my father, like a spirit, could be around here watching me and I'm sure he felt him close to us," but he was afraid he might be laughed at if he blurted this out. What he wanted from Mr. Kemp was some confirmation of his own feeling.

"I mean, dogs can hear sounds we can't hear, isn't that right?" Luke said earnestly. "I've read about high-pitched whistles that men can't hear and dogs can. Why shouldn't they be able to see things we can't see? Sights and sounds. Why shouldn't they, Mr. Kemp?"

"Sights and sounds," old Mr. Kemp said half to himself. "Isn't that alarming, son?"

"Not if things are there to see and hear."

"Angels and unearthly creatures," Mr. Kemp said jokingly. "Well, what did the remarkable Dan see and where?"

"Oh, I don't know, in the woods," Luke began, for Mr. Kemp's smile had put him off. The smile made him feel both lonely and stubborn. He wanted to withdraw with Dan away from the old smiling eyes. "I didn't say anything about Dan seeing angels," he said. "I was just asking a question."

But the smile had gone from the old man's face and, nodding seriously, he reached out sympathetically to the boy, for he knew that he had lost his father and that he was lonely and imaginative. "Go on, Luke," he said. Something in the boy's guarded tone had moved him. "The world is a very strange place, Luke, and there's a lot more in it than meets the eye of a man," he said reassuringly. "Maybe some things meet the eye of a dog that never get into a man's vision. Oh, there are all kinds of powers that we've forgotten thousands of years ago. For instance, Luke, how does a dog find its way home? A sense of direction. A sense of disaster. All big words, Luke. Instinct, that's a word too. You think your own thoughts, Luke, and rely on your own experience."

"I know what you mean," Luke said quickly. He felt he could go on listening forever to this man who could say all the things a boy would like to hear and prove a boy was justified in believing them.

"A boy or a man has to work a lot of things out for himself," Mr. Kemp went on. "That's the way you'll find it, son. Some people never look to the right or the left and only see what's under their noses. Life has no mysteries for them. They're sure of everything. Maybe it's wise not to be too sure about a dog or a man and the spirit that gets into them."

While he had been talking, Mr. Kemp had been stroking Dan's head gently. Then his heavy-veined brown hand encountered Luke's hand, which was holding on to Dan's ear, and they both smiled. "So you see, Luke," he said, "it's hard to say what goes on in this world. You'll have to use your own eyes and your own imagination."

"Sure. That's what I'm going to do," Luke agreed earnestly.

He stayed at the stables with Mr. Kemp until it began to get dark, then they said good night.

Going down the road with Dan, he watched the path of moonlight widening on the bay. They were both tired, and they sauntered along very slowly, Luke dragging his feet, the dog waddling along about a pace behind him. They had had a wonderful time. Now it was good to hear the night birds swooping low and the crickets chirping in the cool grassy ditch. Ahead was the river; from up the river came the soft flowing splash of the dam, and then they were in the big shadow of the silent sawmill, walking in the lights from the windows in the house. And the lights now were friendly, and the whole place was suddenly close to him, for now it seemed that he had begun his own secret satisfactory life with Dan.

8. Learning To Be Practical

Luke began to trail around the sawmill after Uncle Henry, not only because he liked the fresh clean smell of the newly cut wood and the big piles of sawdust and the sound of the saw but because he was impressed by Uncle Henry's precise firm tone when he spoke to the men.

Sometimes Uncle Henry would stand beside Luke at the belt watching the men lifting the cut wood off as the belt moved by slowly. "Yes, sir, they know wood when they see it," he said. "How would you distinguish one piece of wood from another, Luke?"

"Well, first I'd take a look at the color."

"That's good," Uncle Henry nodded. "You're observant all right, and there's the grain, too, remember. The grain's always different and you know something else, Luke? Each kind of wood has its own smell. Just like a perfume. Pick up some of those pieces there, Luke."

"I've noticed there's always a fine smell here," Luke said quickly.

"Smell that hemlock, Luke," Uncle Henry said, holding out a piece of wood. "Isn't it beautiful? And the spruce, too, and the pine. I don't think there's a finer smell in the whole world, Luke. A clean smell, too, isn't it, lad?"

Luke wouldn't have believed that a serious, busy, important man like Uncle Henry would have the time to close his eyes and take a breath and get the fine flavor of the wood; not without feeling he was wasting his time. Maybe he could do it because it was both important and useful to him to recognize each individual odor. It was a part of his business; knowing about these rich fine smells of the different woods made him an expert. If he weren't interested, then he would have gone into some other business. Just the same, the way Uncle Henry closed his eyes and drew in his breath made Luke feel a little closer to him. It was as if he had at last found something in common with him.

Luke spent a lot of time in the mill and he felt happy. And now he hardly ever felt lonely. When he got tired of hanging around the mill he could wander out, whistle softly for Dan, and go trotting off through the woods to the clearing with the big stone; there they would rest awhile and he would think of his father, then play for a while with Dan and be back to the mill in an hour without having to explain where he had been, and feeling somehow more eager to learn whatever Uncle Henry wanted to teach him.

Uncle Henry liked to stop and explain what was useful and what was faulty, and what ought to be thrown away. He always illustrated his point by picking up a piece of timber and saying, "See the grain in that, lad. Look closely," and he would snap the board in his powerful hands. "A bad grain, see. You could tell it at a glance and there's no argument. You've got to know what's useful and what's not useful and learn not to be taken in by the first appearance. That's the great trick, Luke. And the only way to be smart about it is to have the facts at your finger tips. Learn the facts, see, lad? If you've got the facts, you know what's useful and what isn't useful and nobody will ever fool you. Understand?"

"I understand," Luke said, but what he really understood was that it had been a mistake to think he could fool Uncle Henry into believing that Dan was a young dog just by combing him up and primping him and making him dance around. All that he actually had done was make Uncle Henry look at the dog more closely; he had reminded his uncle that Dan wasn't as useful to him as he used to be. Uncle Henry had the facts about Dan. Only it seemed to Luke that his uncle didn't have all the facts; not the facts that he himself had. But these facts he had to conceal from Uncle Henry because they were too hard to explain. Unless you felt them yourself they had no value; they were just like the pieces of wood that Uncle Henry could crack in his hands and throw away.

But Uncle Henry never threw away anything that had any value. Nothing was ever wasted around the mill. Luke used to wonder if there was another man in the world who knew so well what was needed and what ought to be thrown away. It seemed to be the key to a great successful life. If you had that knowledge, then you had a mastery over the life around you. What puzzled Luke was that at home in the city when his father had been alive this knowledge had never been made available to him.

Even around the house or in the kitchen Aunt Helen relied upon Uncle Henry's judgment and sought his approval for all her expenditures. He knew the price of flour, potatoes, sugar, onions, spice, vanilla flavoring, buns, cookies, cuts of beef; he knew just which joints gave you the best value for your money, and exactly how much it cost to run the house for a week. Aunt Helen did not resent his knowledge of what might have been called her affairs because his knowledge seemed to make her life easier. His knowledge was useful to her and she never got cheated. Uncle Henry could even put a price on a bundle of laundry for a woman named Mrs. Ball, who had heavy shoulders and thick arms and gray hair and who used to come to the house three times a week to do the washing and was paid for the amount of washing she did. Uncle Henry could look at the pile of laundry and calculate how long it would take Mrs. Ball to do it: the calculation would be so accurate that Mrs. Ball used to trust Uncle Henry's judgment and be sure she would not be cheated. Sometimes it would be two dollars and fifty cents for the day, sometimes three dollars and twenty cents. But Mrs. Ball knew that Uncle Henry never cheated anybody and counted on no one cheating him.

In the evening Luke would sit in the living room watching his uncle as he sat at his desk making notations in a black notebook. At Luke's feet would be the collie, as motionless as a rug, in fact looking like a skinned wolf because of the posture; his head would be flat on the floor. But his eye would flicker open furtively because the collie seemed to know he was there in the house only because of Luke—was there on borrowed time.

In another chair, the rocker, Aunt Helen would be darning socks. Through the open window came the sounds of the crickets in the grass and the faint sound of the water flowing gently over the dam.

Luke was sharpening a penknife his uncle had given him, drawing the blade slowly back and forth on the oilstone the way Uncle Henry had shown him, his strokes growing slower till finally he stopped and gazed at Uncle Henry with profound attention. Uncle Henry was bending over the table, his great shoulders hunched a little, and sometimes he would look at the ceiling and ponder, then make a note, frown, make a quick calculation, then put his heavy chin on his hand, his elbow on the table. Luke knew that he was assessing the value of the smallest transaction that had taken place during the day.

Luke watched and wondered and began to dream; he seemed to hear himself talking to his uncle, who was saying respectfully, "Here's the way I figure this, Luke. Take a look at this and see if you agree with me."

"If you don't mind my saying so, Uncle Henry, I think your figure is a bit wrong there."

"Oh, you mean these figures here, Luke?"

"That's right." Then with a great clearing of his throat, "Look here, why can't we get rid of all that stuff anyway, Uncle Henry? We don't need it now, do we?"

"Come to think of it, we don't need it now, Luke. What made me think we did?"

"I've been intending to point it out to you, Uncle Henry."

"Don't know what made me figure we really needed it. Say, Luke, I'd like to run over all these figures with you if you have the time. I'd like to take advantage of your good sound judgment if I may."

While he was having this dream his aunt looked up, glanced at the clock and said, "All right, Luke, better be getting to bed."

"Okay, come on, Dan," he said.

Then the collie got up slowly, and with his tail down and a furtive, guilty glance at Uncle Henry, started to follow Luke across the room.

"How is it we let that dog sleep in the house now?" Uncle Henry said suddenly.

"Well, he started doing it the first night with Luke," Aunt Helen explained.

"I thought you said a hundred times, Helen, you weren't going to put up with the hair he sheds around the house. I thought you said he ruined the rugs and Dan was to keep out of the house."

"Well, yes, Henry, I did," she said. Then she glanced at Luke, and hesitated because he looked embarrassed. Dan, his friend, was being humiliated and cheapened: he looked as if he wanted to offer a little apology to the dog. As he turned apprehensively and waited for his aunt to speak, his eyes moved her.

"Until Luke gets to feel a little more at home," she said placatingly, "the dog's a kind of help in that way. It's a help to all of us—for the time being."

"Yes, in that case, I suppose he serves a kind of a purpose," Uncle Henry said thoughtfully. "For a week or so, anyway." Then he turned and smiled a little at Luke, who was waiting apprehensively at the door. "As a matter of fact, Helen," he said. "How do you think Luke's fitting in around here? He looks healthy, doesn't he?"

"I think he's just about right into the swing of things, Henry."

"Yes, yes, I think so. A little inscrutable at times."

"As if all boys of that age weren't inscrutable beyond words."

"A little dreamy perhaps, eh, Luke?"

"Now, Henry, you know Luke's going to be keen as a whistle."

"Yes," Uncle Henry agreed, eyeing the boy approvingly. "In no time we should have him bright as a dollar. Have a good sleep, my boy."

"Good night. Come on, Dan," Luke said. As they went upstairs together he promised himself fervently that as he began to grow Uncle Henry would gain a deep respect for his shrewdness, and that when he was a man everybody would admire him for his good sound judgment.

9. But Tell Me Why

NOTHING was more difficult for Luke than his effort to share his uncle's judgment of the different men who worked in the mill. Sometimes it seemed to him that Uncle Henry didn't understand them at all and had a cockeyed appreciation of the worth and the weakness of each one of them. Of course Uncle Henry judged them all simply as workers and Luke judged them as men.

"That old Sam Carter is a...well, he's a..." Luke began one day at quitting time when the men were filing past on their way home.

"He's a what, Luke?" Uncle Henry asked patiently.

"Oh, I don't know exactly."

"Go on, Luke. How does Sam Carter stand around here in your judgment? You've got to learn to judge workmen. Who knows, some day you may be running the mill. What about my workmen? How does Sam Carter stack up?"

"Well, I'd say he's an awful old dope," Luke blurted out.

"And why, Luke?" Uncle Henry asked patiently.

"The way he goes around,...like a prisoner in a chain gang...with that old beard and those funny old eyes."

"Well, well, well," Uncle Henry said, laughing heartily. "Now there's a boy's innocent view of a very good worker. I'm afraid you're not very observant as yet, Luke," he said seriously. "You want to start pulling up your socks, my boy, and really observe these men."

"Oh, I've observed Sam Carter, Uncle Henry."

"Sam Carter is just about the best worker I've got around here," Uncle Henry explained carefully. "It's up to you, Luke, to see for yourself why this is so. Not that Sam is quick. But he's steady and completely reliable. I've never had any trouble with him. Why, I don't think he ever dreams of anything but his work here at the sawmill. Yes, I judge him by his value to me, not by his lack of beauty. Watch him when he's working, Luke."

"All right, I will," Luke promised.

But no matter how closely he looked at Sam Carter he couldn't understand Uncle Henry's appreciation of him. Maybe Sam knew one kind of wood from another, but only because he had to; he had to recognize the difference in the grain and smell. And even if he did the right thing around the mill he did it in a mechanical way. His eyes never glowed, he never moved quickly or joyfully, he never made much conversation with the other men.

It was always in Luke's mind that Sam Carter had kicked at the collie. He told himself that if he owned the mill he wouldn't want to have Sam Carter working there. A man like Sam Carter would make him feel unhappy. A man like Sam Carter would make him believe that the world was a gray place full of tired, weary men limping along carrying out appointed tasks and seeking only the boss' approval.

Yet the sight of Sam Carter limping along to the mill would stimulate Luke's dream of the place. Luke would sit with Dan in the shade of the elm tree on the north side of the mill watching Sam Carter's slow movements and would delight in dreaming it was a time three thousand years ago, and in this daydream he could see Sam clad in rags, dragging his feet along, carrying his heavy burden without even a heart-rending sigh, for he had long ago forgotten his native land and the days of his boyhood; he was the slave who no longer wanted to be free. Luke liked to pretend he could see him dragging his feet wearily because there were heavy chains on his ankles. And Luke would whisper to Dan, "I know why he hates you, Dan. You're a wild thing. You like to roam the valleys and the woods, and prance around with me and have fun and jump in the river and then sleep in the sun, and the slave hates you for liking these things, Dan."

The old dog, lying in the shade and half asleep himself, blinked his eye knowingly at Luke.

Luke would wonder if he would ever be wise enough to appreciate Sam Carter more than a workman like Alex Malone, that lanky bald-headed mill hand who often stopped for a word with Luke. Alex Malone, whistling to himself, stood with his hands on his hips watching the saws and was always willing to explain something. Yet he did his share of the work, though sometimes he worked a little faster and sometimes a little slower; according to Uncle Henry, Alex Malone was not supposed to be a consistent worker.

Luke also liked a young fellow named Joe Carson, whom Uncle Henry kept an eye on all the time because Joe had had three jobs in the last year; he had worked up north and had been a seaman on the lake boats. Even now he would stand looking out over the bay with a restless expression in his eyes.

"That's one bird of passage, Luke," Uncle Henry had said. "One of these days Joe'll get an itchy foot and he'll be off without as much as a thank-you, and I'll be shorthanded. You can easily figure him out, Luke, and if you're ever in my position, give those fellows a wide berth unless you're stuck. Take a man like old Sam Carter every time."

Luke liked to imagine that he was a little like Joe Carson and would some day get restless and head for the lumber camps in the north woods or sail on the ships. When he had these thoughts he felt guilty; he knew that Uncle Henry would attribute his sneaking admiration for Joe Carson to his inexperience with men.

But there was a fat Pole, Willie Stanowski, with the round happy face and the merry little blue eyes, whom Luke really liked; Willie Stanowski always wore bright red checked shirts. He was a fine workman, quick and intelligent, who had eight children and he lived a mile and a half along the road to town. One of the eight Stanowski children, Tillie, thirteen years old, with ash blonde hair, was in Luke's class in school. She was a pretty and friendly kid.

Luke hadn't heard Uncle Henry say much about Willie Stanowski until one morning when Willie didn't report for work at the mill.

"Luke, hop on your bike and go down to the Stanowski place and find out what's the matter with Willie. Although I could tell what's the matter," he said with a shrug.

Luke got on his bike with Dan following him and went down the road to the Stanowski house, which was well back in a field. It was an old roughcast cottage with a little vegetable patch. The roof of the cottage sagged and patches of roughcast had fallen off the walls. It was one of those places on the outskirts of the town that could be rented for little, for nobody wanted to live there. The place had no shade trees. The grass around the cottage had withered in the sun. An old wheelbarrow, turned over on its side, lay in the path; the woodpile wasn't neat, and there were three clotheslines stretching from the back door of the house, laden with the clothes of the Stanowski children. As Luke turned up the dirt road Willie Stanowski was coming out. Willie looked unhappy. "All right, all right, my boy," he said apologetically. "You come from your uncle, no? Yes, I'm on my way. I hurry. I slept in. I apologize to your uncle."

With a shamefaced grin and walking like a man who had a headache and who was bothered by the sun, he hurried by.

Luke turned to follow him, but Tillie Stanowski called from the door, "Aw, stay a while, Luke, and have some fun."

"What'll we do?" Luke asked. "What kind of fun?"

"Just play around. You know—just have fun."

"Well, I don't know," he said doubtfully. "That's no fun."

"Let's all play with the dog," she coaxed him.

"Dan's a strange dog," he began to explain, but by this time all the Stanowski children were crowding together at the door. Even the little boy, who was only four years old and who had smudges of dirt on his face, was there, and behind him was Maria, the big Stanowski girl who was twenty, and who had on a clean white apron.

"Stay a while, Luke," Maria called cheerfully. She had the largest dark eyes Luke had ever seen, her hair was so black it gleamed in the sun; she was the prettiest girl Luke had ever seen and when she coaxed him to stay he felt important and wanted to stay.

Soon they were having the craziest time he had ever had, for when he and Dan entered the dilapidated house all the children began to chase each other wildly and the dog barked furiously. They chased each other in and out of the house, they knocked over chairs, they bumped into Maria, who was ironing, and she only laughed. And when they were all exhausted little Tillie coaxed Maria to sit down at the old fumed-oak piano which had four broken keys and they all began to sing a favorite French Canadian folk song called "Alouette." They roared, "Alouette, gentille alouette..." And Maria's clear strong voice carried across the field.

"Just wait, just wait," Tillie shouted. "Some day I'm going to be able to sing like Maria."

Luke had never known that running and shouting hilariously and knocking things over could be so much fun, or that Dan could be so energetic; and when he was tired out he found himself wishing he could live for a while with the Stanowskis because he liked Tillie and Maria so much.

So he went back there next day, which was Sunday, and didn't come back to the mill until dinnertime.

After dinner when Uncle Henry was out on the veranda, Aunt Helen, who was sitting in the kitchen with her hands folded in her lap, called, "Just a minute, Luke." She was wearing her new black Sunday dress which made her look like an important woman when she walked down the aisle in church. Now she had a concerned expression. "I don't want you to hang around the Stanowski place, Luke," she said.

"We were only running around," Luke said. "What's the matter with that, Aunt Helen?"

"Well, it's hard to explain, Luke," she went on in a grave tone. "I don't think your uncle would like you hanging around the Stanowski place."

"He never said so to me, Aunt Helen."

"Luke," she said blandly, "when you grow up would you like to be a man like Willie Stanowski or a man like your Uncle Henry?"

"Like my Uncle Henry. Why?"

"Well, of course. You might as well know, Luke, that Willie gives your uncle a lot of trouble." Her voice sinking to a whisper, she added, "Willie Stanowski drinks, Luke. He drinks heavily."

"Oh."

"Yes. It's a shame, isn't it, Luke?"

"I guess it is," Luke said, and he was silent a while pondering over Willie Stanowski's horrible weakness for liquor. Then he suddenly blurted out, "But I don't play with Mr. Stanowski, Aunt Helen. I play with Tillie and I like Maria, too. And they don't drink."

"Yes," Aunt Helen said mysteriously as she went on with her work. "Tillie right now seems to be a nice little thing, Luke."

"She is. Sure, she is."

"A pretty little thing, and you go to school with her, Luke."

"And we're in the same room, Aunt Helen."

"That's exactly it, Luke," Aunt Helen said. She was getting flustered now and having trouble finding the right words, and she hated anything that flustered her. "I don't want you growing up around here feeling too close to any of the Stanowskis, and particularly to Tillie."

"But why?" he asked doggedly.

"Because she'll probably begin to take on a lot of bad habits," Aunt Helen said sharply. "She'll grow up to be like that sister of hers, Maria."

"Maria's a lot of fun, Aunt Helen," he said unhappily. "She sings and plays the piano."

"Yes," Aunt Helen agreed, tightening her lips and flushing. "And she goes places she shouldn't go and sees people she shouldn't see, and gets a bad name and it all means that she'll come to a bad end."

"A bad end? But if she's nice to me, Aunt Helen—"

"Well—"

"Why shouldn't I be nice to her. Why?"

"Oh, for heaven's sake, you're an exasperating child," Aunt Helen snapped at him. Her face bursting red with irritated frustration, she stood up and looked as if she wanted to slap him. To Luke her anger was inexplicable. It was mysterious and irrational; it had never touched him before. "Any stupid child can go on saying, 'Why, why, why?'" she cried.

"But Uncle Henry said I was always to ask why about a thing. He said I should always want to know why."

"Yes," she agreed jerkily. "Uncle Henry would want you to ask 'Why?' about something that could do you some good if you got the answer. The Stanowskis can't do you any good no matter what you know about them, so forget them. Understand, Luke?"

"I understand," he said nervously, although he did not understand. Aunt Helen was a kind woman. In fact, everything she did or said to him was out of kindness; and he knew now that she was thinking of his good. But that was what was most frightening about Uncle Henry and Aunt Helen—their kindness; whatever they did they had the advantage of doing it out of kindness.

He wanted to go back to the Stanowski place but he was afraid of Aunt Helen's anger. It was the kind of anger that would be hard to withstand because it was still inexplicable;

it had to do with her position in the town and in the world and came out of a belief in the rightness of her own kind of life. It would not be like Uncle Henry's anger. Uncle Henry suddenly seemed to be such a safe and solid man. You could count on him. His anger could always be explained. Yet in the classroom at school Luke found himself staring at little Tillie Stanowski, and when she smiled at him he felt ashamed and guilty because her smile was bright and happy, and he couldn't figure out why she was bound to have bad habits while she remained so bright and friendly.

One evening when the lamps were lit in the windows of the houses along the road Luke and Dan approached the Stanowski house. The collie believed that they were going right up to the house, but Luke suddenly said, "No, Dan, stay here." Lying down in the grass he watched the lighted windows of the shabby roughcast house. They were about seventy yards from the house and it was dark. They were hidden from anyone passing in the road or anyone who might come to the door of the house.

But they were close enough to hear the voices of the Stanowski children. Then the moon, suddenly breaking through a bank of clouds, shed its light on the old roughcast house. In a little while there was the sound of the piano, then the sound of Maria's voice, and then singing and laughing.

Lying in the grass and listening, Luke stroked the collie's head and watched the strange forbidden house and was filled with discontent because all the wild happiness contained in that house was never to be touched by him.

Then the collie rose and began to trot toward the house, following the path of moonlight. He turned, waiting for Luke, making a motion with his head, inviting him to follow.

"Come back, Dan," Luke whispered, and the dog returned slowly and reluctantly, but not quite within the reach of his hand.

"We can't go in there, Dan," Luke scolded. But the dog, circling away, backed toward the house, encouraging him to come, and saying with every motion of his body, "Why?"

"I can't explain why," Luke whispered. "Anyway, I don't quite know why, and besides you're a crazy dog and the reason why wouldn't sound any better to you than it did to me. Sit down, Dan. Come on, boy."

All Luke wanted to do was lie there in the dark and listen. But suddenly Dan darted toward the house, swerved and came back, and began to circle around in the moonlight. The collie pranced around in the moonlight swaying and coaxing Luke to follow.

With the sound of the piano and laughter coming from the house, and the old dog circling around in the moonlight, trying to draw him toward the house, Luke began to feel a little crazy himself. Maybe it was the unexpected pallor of the moonlight and the form of the old dog swerving wildly in and out of the light and shadow, but he felt excited and he slowly stood up and watched the dog raptly as if they were both under a spell, and he too would soon begin to dance around in the moonlight.

Believing that Luke was being lured on the collie barked joyously, still circling, going a little faster now. But the dog's sudden bark had upset Luke. He was afraid someone would come to the door. For a moment he remained motionless, staring fixedly at the gleaming windows, then he suddenly turned and started to run toward the road. The dog, stopping his prancing, watched him, let him get about twenty paces away, then relaxed, became a faithful old dog again, and trotted quietly after him.

On the road, going along slowly together, Luke didn't speak to Dan, although he felt apologetic. It was as if he knew that for years afterwards the Stanowskis would live in his mind as a fabulous family, and that whenever he heard a piano in the darkness he would remember that shabby roughcast house with the dog circling in the moonlight and feel restless and discontented.

The next afternoon walking along the road with Dan, he met Maria, who had her hair done with a yellow ribbon, and who was wearing a neat pair of gray slacks. Stopping, she chewed on a blade of grass and looked at him thoughtfully. "You and Dan haven't come back to see us, Luke," she said.

"No. I guess I haven't, Maria."

"The children like the dog. So do I," she said.

"Dan's a very friendly dog," Luke said. "He likes you all a lot. I know he does. Isn't that right, Dan?"

"What's the matter, Luke?"

"Nothing. Nothing," he said uneasily.

Then she behaved very queerly. With an odd smile on her face she stood looking across the road and beyond the bit of marshy ground to the lake, and there weren't even any whitecaps out there, for there was no wind at all. She was looking at the line where the blue sky met the grayness of the water and became one with it, and suddenly she shrugged her shoulders contemptuously. "I won't play around here long," she said. "And neither will Tillie. I'll see that Tillie doesn't stay around here." Her voice was soft as if she had forgotten Luke was there; then she turned and walked down the road and Luke, standing there with the dog, watched her and felt unhappy and mixed up.

10. The Secret World

WHENEVER Luke felt like this it became unbearably hard to go on learning from Uncle Henry. His unpredictable discontent discouraged him. If Uncle Henry had known what was going on in his mind, he would have been disappointed and Luke didn't ever want Uncle Henry to be disappointed in him. Yet he couldn't always be learning from Uncle Henry.

In these restless hours he would lie on his back in the tall cool grass back a piece from the road, the grass so tall he could not be seen, and with Dan beside him he would look at the blue sky and feel a little crazy and think that perhaps God hadn't intended him to be a shrewd and useful man. Then he had to go on building up that secret life he had begun with Dan. It was as if he lived two lives around the sawmill. He was earnest, eager and attentive with Uncle

Henry, but he was only truly happy and not lonely when he was living his secret life with Dan.

They would play around the mill pond where great logs used to float in the old days, and by the dam with its curtain of falling water. It was easy to pretend that the dam was a great waterfall, the pond a harbor, the rowboat a three-masted ship. Luke had built a raft for the pond and used the rowboat on the river. On one side of the pond he built a fortification of old pieces of lumber. This became their pirate lair where he was esteemed as the young lieutenant of Captain Dan, the fierce old one-eyed pirate who raided Spanish galleons and shot up town after town and left a trail of blood along the gulf.

For a while they would lie quietly together, Luke with his hands linked behind his head and his eyes closed. In the familiar dream the pictures raced through his head till he forgot where he was. He could see the river emptying into a great sea, and at the mouth of the river was a harbor with an old castle, and there, lived an unyielding Spanish Don.

He could see the castle overlooking the town's harbor, and the sprawling main street where Negroes and Indians with gold rings in their ears carried baskets of merchandise from the trading ships in the harbor. He could see the helmeted soldiers from the Don's castle loafing along the street or jesting with the golden girls. And within the castle—he could see within the castle very clearly—the Spanish Don was dining at the long oaken table from which he tossed bones to the huge dogs crouching on the rushes on the floor. Luke seemed to see the face of this great burly Don; he weighed over two hundred and thirty pounds and had a brick-red face. It was not that Luke deliberately tried to see in his dream that the Spaniard had Uncle Henry's face; but this Spanish Don was unassailable, his town had never been sacked by pirates because he knew how to arrange his defenses perfectly; he knew what soldiers were needed in one place and weren't needed in another. He couldn't be overcome, because of his vast common sense. Everything for him was always in order. Of all the pirates on the Main this Spaniard hated Captain Dan most of all because of his unpredictable wild life.

"Order, order, we must have some order around here! Make yourself useful," the Spaniard shouted suddenly. "If you're all useful nobody can overcome us."

And in a high-backed chair sat the Don's wife, pink-faced and smelling of talcum powder, and smiling happily every time he gave an order to his men.

There was only one way of overcoming the solid perfection of this great stronghold, by an attack which would be so crazy, unpredictable, wild and frenzied, laughing and drunken that the Spaniard could not plan against it.

Two wild freebooters who understood this secret were there that night in their own sheltered harbor, feasting and drinking and waiting for the dark of the moon. A bronzed damsel who looked like Maria Stanowski was waiting on them. With a great oath Captain Dan suddenly kicked over his chair, yelled for richer wine, and blinked his one amber eye fiercely. There were merchants who shuddered in their dreams, believing that one frightful, yellow eye was gleaming at them in the darkness. Sometimes in their dreams they saw the old one-eyed pirate take the form of a huge dog that went loping over the line of a hill against the moonlight.

And Captain Dan shouted, "Give me my glass, son!" and as he mounted up to the tower they all heard his wild laughter. "I see a Spanish treasure galleon a-sailing up from Panama," he sang hoarsely.

And young Luke the favorite lieutenant chanted, "Row boys, row. Row boys, row."

"Aye, soon we'll be looting it, looting it. Row boys, row," Captain Dan shouted.

Then they rushed to the raft, Dan leading the way and leaping, his cry sounding strangely like the bark of a great dog. Some even said that he looked like a wild dog that had roamed the valleys of the moon. He played up to this idea. In battle he covered himself with a dog skin, and an amber colored fur cap. And there he was now looking strangely like a dog, his cries like the barking of the dog as he shouted his instructions to young Luke. "Push off, son. Heave ho."

"Aye, my Captain," Luke answered proudly. They pushed the raft out on the quiet waters of the great harbor, then they jumped off the raft and crept down to the great waterfall, the frightening roar of tons of water deafening them, and there at anchor was their long rakish craft with the black sails. Captain Dan leaped into the boat. It was that magnificent leap, covered as he was with the skin of a wild dog, that was so frightening; for in the dark of the moon he really became a dog with a glaring yellow eye. As Luke took the oars, Captain Dan stood proudly in the bow of the boat, and they headed downstream toward the great sea which was their domain.

The river widened and on the banks great jagged rocks jutted out with tall trees rising behind the rocks, and in the sunlight, paths through the trees shone with a strange golden light. In the river's shadows and stillness and shimmering light, and just the two of them in the boat with nothing needing explaining and the perfect trust and confidence so completely shared, it was very beautiful.

"Any instructions, Captain Dan?" Luke asked quietly.

But Dan, maintaining his peaceful attitude, only flicked his head as if to say, "Luke, are you asking me for instructions at this hour? After all I've taught you?"

"Then I'm to take the boarding party, Captain?"

"Aye, lad."

"And if there are damsels aboard, Captain Dan?"

"Reserve for me the fairest one to do the chores around the fort. Do no more than box her ears if she makes trouble, a clip on the ear with the open hand, son."

"Aw, Captain Dan, we don't need a damsel around the fort."

"Blast my golden eye, maybe you're right, son."

"I ask a boon. A boon, Captain Dan."

"Name it, Luke. Out with it, you scallion."

"Let's throw the damsels in the sea."

"Aye, throw the damsels in the sea," Dan chanted, and then they both burst into crazy laughter, with Dan's laughter sounding like a bark, and Luke singing happily, "Throw the damsels, the dirty damsels into the sea."

They were now at the mouth of the river with the wide sea blue and shimmering, and over there in the sheltered inlet the galleons were hiding. They beached their boat and Dan, leaping out, waited while Luke drew up the oars. Then they both drew their great swords from their sashes. In the name of Captain Dan, Luke addressed the motley crew who had beached their boats. Night would fall, he said, by the time they crossed through the woods to take the town from the rear. They began the long march.

The sun sank and the moon rose. A wind came up. And when they were camped behind the town watching the lighted windows of the castle, the sea began to moan. In the dark of the moon they converged on the castle. The signal was a wild howl from Captain Dan, and the howl was like a seaborne wail; then they charged. And story-tellers who told about it years later in taverns in strange ports said the charge was like the rush of wolves and wild men that paralyzed with fear the soldiers of the terrible Spanish Don, for the charge was led by a form with a wild, gleaming, yellow eye and it was like a monstrous wild dog. They swore it *was* a dog. But those who knew, only shook their heads sympathetically; they knew it was Captain Dan; and they knew that behind him was his trusted lieutenant, Luke Baldwin, whose sword was as red as blood against the moon. And when they broke into the castle and the retainers were all slaughtered, it was young Luke who faced the burly, two-hundred-and-thirty-pound, red-necked Spaniard; he faced him with a cold superior smile; then he leaped and danced around him like a madman and all the sensible rules of combat the Spaniard knew were of no avail against this frenzy.

With a sudden deft twist of his wrist, Luke sent the blade of the burly Spaniard spinning across the room and it rattled on the stone floor. Thrusting the point of his own blade against the Spaniard's red neck, Luke forced him to his knees. "Mercy!" cried the Spaniard, his great red face full of terror.

"Yes, I'll be merciful," Luke said with a merry laugh. "I'll give you a chance for your life. Get down there on your back. Go on. Get." And as the Spaniard rolled on his back with Luke's blade still pricking at his neck, Luke said, "If you answer a couple of simple questions, I'll spare you."

"Are they riddles?" the Spaniard asked unhappily. "I'm a businessman. Riddles are childish."

"No. I'm after plain facts," Luke said, and the members of the pirate crew who were sitting around in a circle rocked with laughter.

"The question?" the Spaniard asked eagerly.

"All right. Here it is. What color is the deep blue sea?"

"Ah. There's a trick there," the Spaniard said with a cunning smile. "Only I won't be taken in. You see, if I take a little water from the sea and hold it in my hand, why it has no color. It's just water."

"Wrong," Luke said grandly. "The plain fact was right under your nose. I told you it was a deep *blue* sea."

"But I thought that was a trick."

"No, it was such a plain fact you couldn't believe it. All right, one more question."

"I'm ready," the Spaniard grunted with a scowl.

"What's the price of the red feathers on a robin's red breast?"

"Now that's a little difficult," the Spaniard said, closing his eyes as he rested his head on the stone floor. "The trick there is in calling the feathers red and making it seem that red feathers are more expensive than other kinds of feathers. I won't be taken in, though. If I only had my notebook here."

"Go on. Start thinking."

"The only thing such feathers could be used for would be as stuffing for pillows and so on," the Spaniard said profoundly. "Red feathers would be no better than any other kind. If I had my notebook, I'd calculate how much goose feathers cost a pound. I'd figure out the price of a pound of feathers no matter what the color. Look here, can't you have them bring me my black notebook? It's in the pocket of my green doublet."

"What's the use?" Luke jeered. "You're crazy. The red feathers on a robin's breast have no price. They are just something you like looking at and like having around. Anybody knows that. Say, you're kind of dumb, my friend." And with a gesture of contempt he called to three huge pirates, "Take him and put him in chains. Have him grow a beard and let him trail around after us."

And so it was done, and the castle burned and the town wiped out and the galleons looted.

When it was all done there was only the quiet flowing river and the bare sandy beach littered with sun-baked and bleached branches twisted into strange forms; it was like a long strip of desert with the yellow sun-baked branches and logs as smooth as the bones of men who had died in the desert. And it was hot.

Tired now, Luke sat down cross-legged and Dan squatted beside him, his red tongue dripping out and fluttering, his good eye dancing as he waited and puffed and panted.

"That was pretty good, eh, Dan?" Luke said.

The dog flopped down and put his neck on Luke's shoe.

"I hurt my finger when I was pulling the oars in. I kind of crushed it. Look, Dan."

Dan looked and then licked the finger.

"You know something, Dan? Saliva is good for wounds. I read it somewhere. It's a good idea to lick your wounds. Of course, you know that anyway. I had to read it to find out. Well, it's no fun staying here. Come on."

They went down the beach together, taking their time, for now they were just a boy and his dog, and Luke knew where there was a raspberry patch just back beyond the line of trees. When they got to the trees Luke stopped to look up at the heavy vines which were like ropes and he climbed one of the trees and grabbed the vines and swung from one branch to another, wishing there was another boy in the neighbourhood so they could play tree tag. The collie barked and began to make anxious movements with his right front paw. "Okay, Dan," Luke called finally and he jumped down. Then they went into the berry patch where there were three

women and two children picking berries. Circling around
these women Dan barked wildly trying to chase them. They
paid no attention to him, so he settled down beside Luke,
who picked handfuls of raspberries and sat down in the
shade and ate them. Dan ate the berries too. It was remarkable how Dan would eat anything Luke ate.

Luke's hands were stained from the crushed berries; they
were stained as if with blood.

"See that, Dan," he said, holding out his hands. "That's
blood. It's blood on my hands for some great wrong I've
done. We must get to the temple, Dan."

It was cool in the woods and each stone and tree and
trickling brook was part of the one big friendly place. When
they got to the big rock they looked at each other contentedly, but they did not climb to the top. The strong sunlight was hitting the top of the rock. The stone there would
be hot. In a little shaded place where the grass was cool and
green and sweet smelling they lay down to rest and talk.
Luke lay with his head down on his arms, with Dan
stretched out beside him, and while Luke talked, Dan did a
very thorough licking job on the back of Luke's neck. The
long red tongue became like a smooth brush which the dog
applied patiently and exactly with a vast tender concern.

Then Luke began to say things to Dan that he could not
say to his uncle or aunt. Not that what he had to say was
important. It was just stuff about himself that he might have
told to his own father and mother if they had been alive.
"Sleeping in that room of mine is all right, Dan, but I can't
get used to the bed," he said. "Why is a hard bed like that

supposed to be good for a kid's spine? If it's any good for the spine, you'd think, wouldn't you, Dan, that my father would have known about it?"

After brooding a little he said suddenly, "It's a funny thing, Dan, but I'm getting to like Uncle Henry a little more all the time. What I mean is that he's a man you can count on, and he's a kind man, too, and he's never done anything cheap or mean, or a thing that didn't make sense. And I know he likes me, but you probably know that, too, Dan. I think he'd be always there to fall back on if you really needed him. Yeah, that's right. That's Uncle Henry," he said.

Picking a long blade of grass he split it and tried to whistle through it and failed and instead began to chew it, frowning a little. "But you'd wonder, wouldn't you, Dan, that my father and Uncle Henry could be so far apart on what was useful in the world? You didn't know my father, Dan, but he was a man who was always fixing up people who were pretty useless. Old ladies and sick babies, and men who had to lie in bed all the time. I mean invalids. How could those people ever be useful? Why, they were old crocks. Yet my father thought it was important to have them around, and he must have known they were worth something to somebody. See what I mean, Dan?

"But there are some things I don't quite get the hang of, Dan," he went on. And as if Dan had said, "What things, Luke?" he explained, "Well, it's this business of what's useful or valuable and what isn't. I don't see how Uncle Henry gets it straight so easily." He pondered over these matters, asking himself why it was of no value to Uncle Henry that the blue mountains were blue. Nor would Uncle Henry agree that Dan had any value. Even the fleecy clouds overhead in the sky that he liked watching had no real value, and the sound of the rain on the water which was often so fascinating to him was of no worthwhile significance. And Maria Stanowski, who seemed to him to be such a kind-hearted laughing girl, was supposed to be worthless. It was all pretty complicated; the things that made his life entertaining and often magical were the useless things according to Uncle Henry. Luke sighed and wondered how long it would take him to be wise enough to judge truly of what was really important in the world.

11. The Trials of a New Kid

THE old dog helped Luke get better acquainted with the boys at school and particularly with Elmer Highbottom, the son of the rich merchant who had Uncle Henry's approval. Luke himself was too reticent and too quiet; he spoke too politely, and so the other boys jeered at him and would not believe he was really one of them. But the dog was always with him when he showed up at the ball field behind Stevenson's orchard; the boys would talk with the dog and play with him and compare him with Elmer's dog which was also supposed to be a thoroughbred.

Elmer was a skinny red-haired kid, two years older than Luke, who had become the leader of the boys by the power of his abusive voice and his frantic bad temper. Of course, all the kids argued in loud jeering tones, but Elmer could scream and jeer and swing his arms more passionately than the others.

They all wanted to be big league ballplayers, and Elmer had decided that he would become a great left-handed pitcher. One way of being friendly with Elmer was to stand behind him when he was pitching and say, "Wow, did you see that curve? How did you throw it, Elmer?"

Luke, who was lonely and wanted to have friends, would stand behind Elmer, and one day he said enthusiastically, "Boy, what a hook you had on that one, Elmer." It made him a little sick at his stomach to say it, for the ball didn't curve at all; but he wanted Elmer's friendship and he would have liked to believe that Elmer would some day be a great ballplayer.

All Elmer really had was a first baseman's mitt. When he was pitching he used this first baseman's mitt and when a ball came his way he stuck the glove down like a broom and hoped the ball would stick in the pocket. For another thing, he insisted on wearing a fancy rainproof cloth hat, like a man's felt hat, which his father had bought in the city. Luke couldn't imagine a pitcher, even a left-hander with red hair, ever amounting to anything when he wanted to pitch wearing a hat like that one.

But the day Luke said wistfully, "I wish you'd show me how to throw that great curve of yours," Elmer thawed and became friendly and took Luke home with him to show him his valuable thoroughbred dog.

There are several breeds of collie dog, some big and some smaller, but as soon as Luke saw this dog, Thor, which was chained up at a kennel at the back of the big Highbottom house, he doubted that the dog was a thoroughbred. Its legs

were too long; it didn't have the long-haired coat of a collie;
the hair was more like that of an Alsatian; but it was a big,
powerful, bad-tempered dog which was always kept on a
leash.

"It's a thoroughbred," Elmer said, "and it can lick any dog
in this town."

"If that dog's a thoroughbred, then our Dan isn't," Luke
said.

"Then your Dan isn't. This is a fighting thoroughbred."

"Aw, go on," Luke said.

"Aw, go on yourself. Nuts to you."

"Nuts to you, Elmer. Why has it got that crazy look in
its eyes?"

"Because it doesn't like strangers, see, and it doesn't like
other dogs," Elmer said.

But then Mr. Highbottom came out of the house. He was
a plump, affable, sandy-haired man with rimless glasses and
a round pink face and he talked cheerfully with Luke about
Thor. He had a great deal of assurance and a pleasant little
smile, and his clothes were expensive, and there was no
doubt about his being a rich man, and a good friend of
Uncle Henry's. When Elmer went into the house to get his
new first baseman's glove, Mr. Highbottom explained that
Thor was kept as a watchdog; he had got the dog from
some people in the city who had kept it locked up in an
apartment and it was too big to be locked up like that; it
had been badly treated. The first night he, Mr. Highbottom,
had got it he had had to hit it on the head with a club to
let it know who was master. It was half collie and half

Alsatian and a wonderful dog to have around the place at night as a protection against tramps and burglars.

When Elmer came out of the house, Luke said nothing about knowing the dog was not a thoroughbred; he wanted to keep Elmer's friendship.

All the bigger boys at school were friends of Elmer's and now Luke could trail along with them after school and in the evenings. He would go home after school and get Dan and then walk back to the field where they played ball. He had no real influence with Elmer and no influence with Elmer's friends, for he couldn't get used to that technique of abuse which was Elmer's effective weapon. Elmer would scream, "You dope, you great big dope. You lunkhead," and get his way even with the boys who were his own size.

In the gang there were six of them; Eddie Shore, the dark and muscular son of a grocer; Woodie Aliston, the undertaker's son; Jimmie Stewart, the minister's boy; Dave Dalton, the left-handed first baseman, whose father owned the ice-cream parlor; Hank Hennessey, whose father worked in the shipyard; and Norm McLeod, whose father was the superintendent of the grain elevator.

If they were playing ball and Luke missed a fly ball, Elmer, the potential big leaguer, would scream at him in derision and Luke secretly hated him. Lying in the grass by the third-base line with Dan, Luke would whisper, "He's a one-armed ballplayer himself. He just swings that glove at the ball, Dan. If the ball sticks in the pocket, he's all right."

He was not afraid of Elmer, but he never said these things to him; he wanted to go on hanging around with the boys.

In the evenings they would all go up to the fair grounds, especially if a team from one of the grain boats in the harbor was playing the town team. The players on a ship's team came from cities like Chicago, St. Louis and Detroit, and the kids believed that each one of them was a major league ballplayer. Luke was always ill at ease because he didn't even know the members of the town team; he couldn't stand behind the bench when the home team was batting and chat and kid with these great players.

So he would listen, or wander among the crowd, with Dan following him, or he would drift out to left field where the gang would sprawl in the grass. The collie never followed Luke ostentatiously. Anyone watching would hardly have believed that the dog belonged to Luke, who never turned and called to him. Nor would anyone have believed that the collie was intent on being with Luke. Yet if the boys got up to go, the dog, though apparently sleeping, would get up quietly and trail after them. Though Luke and Dan seemed to pay no attention to each other, each knew without looking where the other was; each was aware of what the other was doing.

Dan seemed to know that Luke resented Elmer Highbottom. Luke had it figured out that if Elmer Highbottom had treated him with more respect, the other boys would have willingly let him become truly one of them. If they were lying in the grass having an argument about whether bats were harmless and if Luke was insisting that he had read that bats wouldn't even touch a woman's hair, Elmer would jeer, "Aw, Luke doesn't know anything about it.

How could he know what goes on? He's green. He only knows what he reads in a book. He's just got a lot of sissy talk."

Sometimes Elmer would whisper with Eddie Shore, the swarthy and muscular son of the grocer, and they would go off by themselves, planning some night adventure on the main street of the town. As Luke and Dan walked along the road home with the stars coming out and the night breeze rustling through the leaves of the great elms along the road, he would ache with discontent and try to imagine that he was following the boys furtively into mysterious places where he had never been; he seemed to hear conversations and dark whispering he had never heard before.

But on Saturday mornings it was really worth while to be with Elmer's friends, for then they would go down to the old dock by the rusty grain elevator, and go out to the end of the pier where rotting beams stuck out of the water. There they would swim, the old collie swimming with them, and afterwards they would lie in the sun, talking and dreaming, and after they had dressed they would go along the pier to the place where the Missouri was tied up and sit there peering into the darkness of the hold.

A seaman, in a torn black sweater whose face was leathery and whose hair was iron gray, was sitting on the pier smoking his pipe. He was taking it easy, enjoying the sun and the cool breeze from the water, and smiling to himself as he watched Elmer Highbottom strutting around. A lot of men made a mistake about Elmer. They believed he was high-spirited, a battler, a reckless red-haired kid with blazing blue eyes. And this seaman called to Elmer, "Heh, kid, how old are you?"

"Thirteen. Why?" Elmer asked.

"Oh, nothing," drawled the sailor. "It's just that I remember when I was thirteen around here."

"Are you from around here, Mister?"

"Believe it or not," the sailor said. "I was a kid around here. It was a long time ago," he said, and now he seemed to belong to many other places, but he had been born in the town; a few weeks after his thirteenth birthday he had had a row with his father and one night he had sneaked out the window and come down to this dock and had stowed away on a grain boat.

Both Luke and Elmer, sitting cross-legged now at the seaman's feet, listened to him telling stories about his adventures. He had sailed on the high seas; he had gone down the St. Lawrence; twice on the Pacific his ship had gone down; he had spent a winter in Tahiti; once he had made a voyage to Bangkok; but of all the water of the world these fresh waters of the great lakes were the most like home.

Maybe he was lying a little, but his voice was soft, his tone full of affection and his eyes happy, and so Luke believed him. And after a profound silence Luke said suddenly, "I could do that too. I could stow away some night. I could go down the St. Lawrence. I could sail to Siam."

"When are you going to make the break, son?" the sailor asked with a smile.

"One of these nights. I'll pick a night."

"You," Elmer jeered in derision. "Listen to him, Mister.

He's never been on a ship. He doesn't know one end of a ship from another. He's just a punk around here."

"I was a punk once," the sailor said in such a way that Luke felt grateful. "Maybe the lad's got the stuff," he went on looking thoughtfully at Luke, who was blushing and scowling at Elmer for so brutally belittling him.

"I guess I know what I've got," he said belligerently to Elmer. Luke couldn't figure out why he endured Elmer's jeering insults. He would say to himself bitterly, "I despise him. I don't take anything he says seriously, and neither does anybody else." But if he turned against Elmer, he would be turning against the other boys too; he felt too insecure to be against them all. And gradually they had all adopted Elmer's tone with him. Lacking confidence he had become hesitant and felt lucky to be allowed to go along with them.

Even though he was a city kid he longed to be able to show them there was nothing he was afraid to do, if they would do it also. When they were crossing the freight yards they would all stand waving at the brakemen, all dreaming of being on the train which would carry them away to strange cities. Sometimes one of the boys would yell, "I'll stump you to take a ride." "Stumpers go first," someone would yell, and the kid would rush at the slow-moving freight and grab at the ladder leading up to the car roof; one by one the kids would jump at these ladders, and Luke was never the last one. With his heart pounding and the smell of cinders in his nostrils and the earth shaking under his feet as he ran, he would hang on tight to the ladder and scream encouragement to Dan, who tore alongside barking hysterically. As the train began to pick up speed, they would jump off one by one.

One day they were in Johnson's lumberyard on the south side of the tracks, playing around the great pile of sawdust which was heaped at the back of a two-story brick building. A ladder hooked to the wall of the building ran up to the flat roof. "Come on, all up on the roof," Elmer yelled, and they followed him up the ladder.

Sitting on the edge of the roof they all looked down at the pile of sawdust which was about twenty feet below. The collie down there, looked up at them expectantly.

"I'll stump you to jump down," Elmer said, and without waiting for them to yell, "Stumpers go first" he jumped off the roof, rolled over in the pile of sawdust and got up shaking the golden dust out of his red hair and grinning triumphantly. "Who's next?" he yelled.

One by one the boys began to jump, and as each one fell Dan barked excitedly. But the second boy to jump had taken a little longer to make up his mind and the third boy hesitated even longer, the jump becoming longer and more frightening as he kept looking down; and Luke, who was the last one, had had too much time to think about it. Elmer had made the jump easily and nervelessly; he had given himself no time to think about it. Now Luke sitting there alone on the edge of the roof hesitated while the others grinned up at him.

"Come on, Luke," they yelled.

"What's the matter with you, Luke? What are you scared of?"

"I'm coming. What's the rush? Why are you trying to rush me?"

"Don't take all day. We're going home."

"I'm taking my time. What's the matter with taking my time?"

He wanted to jump, he knew he was going to jump, only he couldn't bring himself to do it at the moment. It wouldn't hurt him to jump. It was really an easy jump, so he laughed and tried to keep on kidding with them; but he had tightened up and every time he got ready, a queasy feeling came at the base of his spine. Feeling ashamed, he sat there staring at the sawdust pile, wondering why he couldn't force himself off the roof. All he needed, he kept telling himself, was a little more time.

The collie looking up at him wagged his tail expectantly and suddenly gave three eager barks. Luke only frowned.

"I think he's yellow," Elmer shouted. "He's got glue on his pants. Sure, he's yellow. Aren't you yellow, Luke?" Then they all began to jeer, and Elmer shouted, "Sure, look at his old dog. The old dog knows Luke's yellow. The old dog is trying to coax him down. The old dog would like to do it for him."

The jeering excited Luke, and he was hating Elmer so much that he began to tremble; he wanted to close his eyes and jump but was ashamed to let them see that he was closing his eyes. That all this was happening bewildered him. And then the collie began to bark impatiently. "Okay, Dan," Luke yelled, and he waved his arms carelessly as if he had been only kidding them. Then suddenly he pushed himself blindly off the roof and fell heavily on the sawdust and the dog leaped at him joyfully.

"Well, there you are loudmouth," he said to Elmer as he got up, dusting his clothes.

"Who's a loudmouth?"

"You've got the biggest loudest mouth in this town, Elmer," Luke said quietly. "You're a blowhard. A great big loudmouthed blowhard."

"Listen, punk, you want something?"

"You don't worry me, loudmouth."

"You want I should smack you, you stinker?"

"Go ahead and smack me, Elmer. I'll show you who's a stinker."

"You heard that, guys? He wants I should smack him. You heard him," Elmer cried.

"Okay, Elmer, smack him," Eddie Shore said.

"Wait a minute," Elmer said. Looking around on the ground he picked up a chip of wood and balanced it on his shoulder. "Come on, knock it off, you stinker. Come on."

"Knock it off yourself, loudmouth," Luke said.

"You're too yellow to knock it off."

"Wait a minute," Eddie Shore said, with a judicial air. Taking the chip from Elmer's shoulder he put it on Luke's shoulder. "Maybe you should knock it off, Elmer," he said profoundly.

With a scowl Elmer studied the stick which was balanced so delicately on Luke's shoulder, and seemed to be weighing the legal aspects of the assault, or to be wondering if Luke would really hit him if the chip was knocked from his shoulder. For a moment Elmer was in the position Luke had been in when he had been hesitating on the roof, and delaying doing a thing he knew he could do. Suddenly, with a derisive snarl, he swept the chip from Luke's shoulder. "Come on," he yelled.

Then they were circling around each other and now Luke was happy. It was a crazy kind of happiness; it seemed as if Elmer had been pounding him for a long time and now at last he could openly smack Elmer. As they feinted at each other, Dan began to growl. Eddie Shore grabbed him by the collar and held him.

Impressed by the wild glare in Luke's eyes, Elmer feinted cautiously and then suddenly he ducked and charged, swinging his right, and Luke blindly stuck out his left hand like a rod. Elmer walked right into it. The fist got him on the nose, which spurted blood. Stooping, he put his hand delicately to his nose, looked astonished as he saw the blood on his fingers, and then screaming like an old woman he came clawing at Luke and got his arms around him and they rolled in the sawdust. He was heavier and stronger than Luke and had got on top of him.

"Let him up. Let him up and go on fighting," the others yelled. But Elmer, frantic now, his freckled white face with the mouth gaping open and a trickle of blood from his nose running into the corner of his mouth, had grabbed Luke by the hair and kept banging Luke's head on the ground and digging his knees into his ribs while his friends tried to pull him off. And Luke was stunned and bewildered by Elmer's crazy sobbing.

The collie had growled; he lay back growling, then suddenly he jerked his head free and leaped at Elmer. He didn't look like a wild dog, but like a dog being workmanlike. He slashed at Elmer's leg; only at the cloth, but the growl and the sound of the ripping cloth seemed to jerk Elmer out of his frenzy. He was scared. Jumping up, he shouted, "I'll kill that dog. I'll brain him. Where's a brick, somebody?"

"Come here, Dan. Come here quick," Luke cried. As the dog turned to him he grabbed him by the ruff. "You're not hurt," he said to Elmer. "It's only your pants torn a little. Dan didn't bite you."

"I'll brain that dog," Elmer shouted. "I've got a right to kill him now."

"If you want to hit somebody, come on, hit me now I'm standing up. Here," he said to Eddie Shore. "You hold Dan—and hold him this time."

"I'll get you when your vicious dog isn't with you," Elmer yelled. "I'll get you after my father has that dog destroyed."

"You can get me any time you want, Elmer. I'll fight you any time you're willing to have a fair fight."

"Aw go on, beat it. Do you hear? Beat it."

As Luke dusted himself off, taking a long time, he waited for one of the other boys to make a friendly remark, or invite him to stay with them. But they had all grown profoundly meditative. They were all uneasy with one another. So finally Luke said, "Come on, Dan," and he went off by himself.

Cutting across the railroad tracks he started down the road home, and the dog, keeping close beside him, refused to be distracted by birds in the hedges or sounds in the ditches. They were both quiet and concerned. Luke's head began to ache; he felt dizzy; his head had been pounded on the ground; there was a soreness in his scalp in the place where Elmer had tried to tear the hair out by the roots.

After walking on silently for a quarter of a mile he said suddenly to Dan, "A loudmouth like Elmer is apt to say anything to his father. He's apt to go home and tell his father that you bit him, Dan, and Mr. Highbottom is a friend of Uncle Henry's, and that means trouble for you, and I don't know how much trouble Uncle Henry thinks you're worth." What Luke was saying had no meaning for the dog, who knew nevertheless that Luke was worried; he kept glancing up at him, wanting him to go on talking.

Luke got home just in time for dinner and when he was sitting at the table his aunt, noticing a scratch on his face, said, "Is that a scratch on your face, Luke? How did you scratch your face?"

"We were playing up in the lumber yard, jumping in the sawdust, Aunt Helen."

"What fun is there jumping in sawdust, Luke?"

"Oh, it's something to do. You just jump, and you hit the sawdust."

"Why would anyone want to jump in sawdust? Who were you with, Luke?"

"Elmer Highbottom."

"Oh. That's nice. You're becoming great friends, aren't you," she said approvingly.

"Yeah," he said. "We're getting to know each other."

After dinner he sat down in the armchair in the corner and watched Uncle Henry making notes in the black notebook. Uncle Henry, in his shirt sleeves, big-faced, thin-haired, thoughtful now, his great shoulders hunched over the table, looked as if he had the strength of character to protect fearlessly everything that belonged to him; and Luke, watching him furtively, longed to reach out to him and claim that protection; but he seemed to see Mr. Highbottom coming into the room and explaining that the collie had bitten his son. Luke could almost hear them talking as one practical man to another, and coming finally to a practical arrangement. If Uncle Henry could only understand that the fight with Elmer was inevitable, if he could only understand that Dan had intervened out of love, and that such love was important and practical because it was a part of their life at the mill!

And he kept on watching and telling himself Uncle Henry was a man who loved the sweet smell of wood. The kind of reliable man he could count on to protect Dan against a rich man like Mr. Highbottom. Suddenly Uncle Henry looked up; their eyes met; Uncle Henry smiled; feeling embarrassed Luke said quickly, "I guess I'll go up and help Mr. Kemp round up the cows."

12. *The Valiant Hearted*

Bᴜᴛ no complaint came to Uncle Henry from Mr. Highbottom, and at school Elmer was as nonchalant with him as if nothing had happened. On Friday afternoon Eddie Shore, Elmer's good friend, said to Luke, "Going to play ball tomorrow morning, Luke? Guess we'll see you there, eh?"

"Sure, I'll be up there," Luke said with a grateful grin.

That Saturday morning at about ten o'clock he walked up to the ball field with Dan. When he got there he found only two other kids waiting, Eddie and Woodie Aliston, the undertaker's son. It was a cloudy morning and looked like rain; in fact it had rained a little early in the morning, so Luke assumed the other boys would show up later.

While Dan lay under the hawthorn tree, Luke and Eddie and Woodie played three-cornered catch. Then the sun came out weakly. It looked as if the grass would dry and it would be a clear day. If the sun shone brightly, soon all the other kids would come to the field.

"Here comes Elmer now," Eddie Shore said laconically.

"Soon they'll all be here," Luke said. Feeling a little embarrassed about Elmer, he did not turn to watch him coming across the field. But Eddie, who had the ball, held on to it as he looked across the field; and he had such a big excited grin on his face that Luke turned to see what made him so happy.

Elmer was coming toward them and with him was the big dog, Thor, on a chain, and the powerful dog was tugging and pulling Elmer along so that he had to lean back with his weight against the pull on the chain.

"Why has he got that dog?" Luke asked. "Why, that's a crazy dog." Then his heart beat came up high in his throat and he felt weak, for now he knew why Eddie Shore had grinned and why he had been asked to come there that morning. "Come here, Dan," he called quickly. As the old dog came slowly to him he whispered, "You stay right here with me, Dan. No matter what happens you stay here with me."

Elmer, who was close to them now, had on a short-sleeved blue sweater and a pair of khaki pants, and he was grinning exultantly. The sight of Luke there with Dan beside him fitted perfectly into the plan Elmer had worked out, and the big dog with the wicked crazy eyes had already growled at Dan, who was waiting apprehensively. Thor was three inches higher and years younger than Dan and he hated everybody.

"I see you've got your dog with you, Luke," Elmer said with a smirk.

"Yeah, Dan's always with me, Elmer."

"That dog of yours is a mighty savage dog," Elmer said softly. "It goes around biting people, doesn't it?"

"Dan's not savage. Dan never bit anybody."

"Of course, I'm nobody. A dog that bites me isn't really a savage dog. That's not the way I heard it, eh, guys?" With a grin he turned to Eddie Shore and Woodie Aliston, but they did not grin, for now that they were close to Thor and having heard him growl, they were frightened.

And looking into Thor's eyes, Luke realized what a crazy dog he really was; for the eyes, half yellow and half green, had no expression in them; they were like glass eyes, reflecting the light, only you couldn't look into them. Dan's one amber eye was soft and gentle like a deer's; you could go on looking into it, seeing into Dan's heart and liking what you saw, but this big dog's eyes, because they were so bright and empty, were frightening.

"You better take that dog home, Elmer," Luke said placatingly. "Your father told me he was never to be let off the leash. I don't think your father would like it if he made trouble for anybody."

"Is that a fact?" Elmer said mockingly.

"What do you think you're going to do, Elmer?"

"I'm going to see if that dog of yours wants to growl and bite when there's another dog around," Elmer jeered. Slipping the chain off Thor's collar, he pointed to Dan, "Go get him, boy," he yelled. "Sic him."

"Grab him, Elmer. Please, please, grab him," Luke cried out in a desperate anguished protest.

Thor had growled, his lips trembling and drawing back from the long white teeth; he growled a little as Dan stiffened, then growled again, his mane rising. And Dan, too, growled, his head going down a little, waiting, and showing his teeth which were blunted and old.

Suddenly Thor leaped at Dan's throat, trying to knock him over with the weight of the charge and sink his teeth in the throat and swing him over and kill him as if he were a rat.

But Dan pivoted, sliding away to the side, and Thor's snapping jaws missed the throat. For the moment, Dan became a thoroughbred whose life was in danger. His stiff leg, his one eye, his worn teeth were forgotten, as he drew on the ancient strength and wisdom of his breed; his strength was all instinct and heart, and it was against that instinct to snap or chew, or grip with his teeth and snarl and roll over clawing and kicking and cutting until it was over. As Thor missed, Dan did not back away and wait again. Doing what he would have done five years ago, he wheeled, leaping past the big dog and slashing at the flank; then, wheeling again, returned for another slashing rip.

These splendid, fearless movements were executed so perfectly that Luke sobbed, "Oh, Dan," but the slashes at Thor's flank had not gone deep; they were not painful; they only mystified and infuriated the big gleaming-eyed dog.

The sun, which was now bright, was shining in Thor's wild empty eyes. Growling and scraping at the ground with his claws, he charged again; this leap was like the pounce of a great cat. But again the snapping jaws missed Dan's throat, although this time Dan could not slip away; the weight of the charge catching him on the hip spun him around off balance and bewildered him a little because he had counted on being nimble and being ready for his own sudden wheel and slash; his muscles hadn't responded quickly enough; he backed away, bewildered a little.

Luke was watching with both his hands up to his face; it was as if he was prepared to cover his eyes and scream but couldn't; he was frozen to the one spot in an unbelieving trance. The two boys, Eddie Shore and Woodie Aliston, were close together, crouching a little and crazy with excitement. But the wide grin had gone from Elmer's face; his jaw was moving loosely and he kept blinking his eyes.

The thin clouds overhead broke up and a blue patch of sky appeared, and the sun shone brightly on the damp grass and it glistened on the wet leaves of the hawthorn tree.

Thor had learned now that Dan was vulnerable on the left flank; the blind eye saw nothing, the good eye couldn't shift quickly enough. Whirling quickly, Thor charged in again on that left flank, knocking Dan over, but the weight of his own charge caused Thor to sprawl over Dan; the teeth could only snap at the flank, and though both dogs had rolled in the grass, snarling and clawing, Dan was soon on his feet again.

But Dan knew now that something was wrong; he knew that his instinctive style was no good; he couldn't move fast enough and he was bleeding just behind the shoulder. When this heavy dog came whirling to the left of him, he couldn't see him in time.

It was like watching a bewildered old dog suddenly becoming aware of his age, and yet with courage trying to break itself of a style of fighting which was the only one its breed had known for hundreds of years; he was groping dimly by instinct for some way of accepting his handicap and using effectively whatever strength he had until he died.

Circling and backing he drew near the trunk of the hawthorn tree; there he stood with the tree on his left, protecting that flank, so that Thor would have to charge toward the good eye.

There he was prepared to die if he had to and die hard, and this resolution was revealed in the droop of his head and the way he waited, and all the boys saw it.

"No, oh, no, Elmer," Eddie Shore said weakly.

"Elmer. Have some sense, Elmer," Woodie Aliston pleaded.

"Elmer," Luke shrieked suddenly, and he grabbed Elmer by the throat. "I'll kill you. I'll kill you. Call him off or I'll kill you," he shrieked.

But with a low exultant growl, Thor had leaped in again to pin Dan against the tree. Again he missed the throat as Dan swerved a little but he got his teeth in the shoulder, snarling and worrying, shaking his head as he rolled Dan over, shaking and stretching his neck away from Dan's teeth, and holding on tight till he could draw Dan underneath him on his back and then shift his jaws to Dan's throat and kill him.

The agonized growling and snarling was terrible and yet exultant and Luke screamed again, "Elmer! Elmer, oh, please call him off! He'll kill him, Elmer," but he had let go his hold on Elmer for he couldn't take his eyes off Dan.

And the other two boys, Eddie Shore and Woodie Aliston, awed and sick, yelled, "Do something, Elmer. Don't let him kill him, Elmer."

Elmer was fascinated by the power and viciousness of his dog, which he believed he couldn't control.

While he was sobbing, Luke realized all that Dan had meant to him. It was as if Dan was more than a dog; the collie seemed to have come out of that good part of his life, the part he had shared with his own father. Dan had come to share his life with him and understand what was truly important around the sawmill and help him to join this new life with the old good life.

"Dan! Dan!" he screamed. He looked around wildly for help. On the other side of the tree was a thick broken branch. It flashed in his mind that he should use this branch as a club; this was in his mind as he rushed at the snarling dogs. But instead he kicked at Thor's flank; he kicked three times with the good heavy serviceable shoes Uncle Henry had bought for him.

Thor snarled, his head swinging around, his eyes bright with hate on Luke, the lip curled back from the fangs. Luke backed away toward the club. As he picked up the branch and held it with both hands, he felt numb all over; there was nothing but the paralyzing beat of his own heart; nothing else in the world.

Seeing him there with the club, Thor tried to hold Dan down with his paws, then he suddenly growled as he let go of Dan's shoulder and whirled on Luke.

"Luke, come away from him," Elmer screamed.

"Run, Luke," Eddie Shore yelled. "Get someone at Stevenson's, Woodie."

Woodie Aliston started to run across the field to Stevenson's house as Luke, waiting, watched Thor's trembling lip. The big dog's growl was deep with satisfaction as he came two steps closer, the head going down.

In Luke's mind it was all like a dream; it was like a dream of Mr. Highbottom telling him he had once pounded Thor on the head with a club and of a story he had once read about Indians pounding the heads of wild dogs with clubs. But it was important that he should not wait, that he should attack the dog and cow him.

Dan, free now, had tried to get up and then had fallen back and was watching him with his glowing eye.

With a deep warning growl Thor crouched, and Luke rushed at him and cracked him on the skull, swinging the club with both hands. The big dog, trying to leap at him, knocked him down, and when he lurched and staggered to his feet, Thor was there shaking his head stupidly, but still growling. Not waiting, Luke rushed at the dog and whacked him on the head again and again. The crazy dog would not run; he was still trying to jump at him; suddenly he lurched, his legs buckled, and he rolled over on his side.

While Elmer and Eddie Shore were looking at him as if they were afraid of him, Luke did a thing he hated himself for doing. He went over and sat down beside Dan and put his hand on Dan's head and then he started to cry. He couldn't help it; it was just relief; he felt weak and he ground his fists in his eyes.

"Whew, Luke," Elmer said in relief, "you might have got killed."

"Good night! Luke," Eddie said softly. "Are you all right?"

"You better put the chain on that dog of yours, Elmer," Luke said when he could get his breath. "You'd better tie him up to the tree."

"Maybe he's dead. Oh, Luke, what if he's dead?"

"Not that dog. Not that crazy dog. It's Dan that's hurt."

When Elmer was linking the chain to his collar, the dog's legs trembled convulsively. Opening his eyes he tried to get to his feet, but Elmer had no trouble dragging him over to the tree and looping the chain around the tree.

Across the field at the gate to the Stevenson house, Mr. Stevenson was talking with Woodie Aliston. They could see him point and shrug; there seemed to be no trouble over there by the tree; then he turned back to the house and Woodie came on alone.

"Let's see your shoulder, Dan," Luke said gently to the collie lying quietly beside him. The collie knew he had been hurt, knew the muscle above the shoulder was torn and bleeding, yet he lay there quietly and patiently, regaining his strength while his flanks heaved. The good eye was turned to Luke. The collie wanted to rest a little, and then look after the wound in his own way, and with his intelligent amber eye he was trying to convey this to Luke.

"Okay, okay," Luke said softly. Taking out his handkerchief, he dabbed at the blood already congealing on the fur. The other three boys, kneeling down beside Luke, were silent; sometimes they looked at Luke's white face. When he had mopped up the blood, he began to stroke Dan's head softly and Dan, wiggling his tail a little, thumped the grass three times as if saying, "Leave me alone a few minutes, Luke. I'm all right."

"Maybe he's not hurt so bad," Elmer said nervously, for Dan, swinging his head around, had begun to lick the wound patiently; the clean pink tongue and the saliva on the tongue were cleaning and soothing the slash. The tongue was like a doctor's medicinal sponge being used after surgery; and Luke and the other boys seemed to be waiting for Dan to come to a conclusion about the seriousness of his wound.

"Can you get up, Dan?" Luke whispered. "Come on, try."

Slowly the collie rose and hobbled on three legs in a little circle, the wounded right leg coming down delicately and just touching the ground, as he completed the little circle. Coming over to Luke, who was kneeling and waiting anxiously, the old collie rubbed his nose against Luke's neck, then flopped down again.

"I guess he'll be all right, won't he?" Elmer asked anxiously.

"Maybe that leg won't be so good again," Luke said mournfully. "Maybe it'll never be good again."

"Sure it will, if nothing is broken, Luke," Elmer insisted. As he got up he thrust his hands into his pockets and walked around aimlessly, his freckled face full of concern. Once he stopped and looked at his own dog, which was crouched by the tree, his eyes following Elmer. Thor was a subdued dog now. Growing more meditative and more unhappy, Elmer finally blurted out, "I guess you'll tell your uncle what happened, eh, Luke?"

"You knew Dan was my uncle's dog," Luke said grimly.

"If you tell your uncle, well, your uncle will tell my father, and then there'll be awful trouble, Luke."

"Well, you knew there'd be trouble, Elmer."

"I only wanted to scare you and chase Dan," Elmer insisted. "I thought Dan would run and howl. I didn't know Thor would turn on you. Oh, Luke, I was crazy. I didn't stop to think." With a sudden pathetic hopefulness he muttered, "I could have told my father that your dog slashed at me. Only I didn't, Luke. I didn't say anything though he asked me how I tore my pants."

"Okay, you didn't say anything, Elmer. So what?"

"Maybe if you don't say anything...eh, Luke?"

"Aw, I can look after myself, too," Luke said grandly.

"Well—well—in that case I'd sure think you were a great guy, Luke," Elmer said fervently.

"Sure, he's a great guy," Eddie Shore agreed firmly.

Eddie and Woodie Aliston wanted to make friendly gestures to Luke, and they didn't quite know how to do it. They felt awkward and ashamed. They took turns petting Dan lovingly. They asked Luke if he wouldn't go swimming down at the dock after lunch. "I'll walk home with you, Luke," Eddie said.

"I'm not letting him walk all that distance," Luke said, and he knelt down, gathered Dan in his arms and hoisted him up on his shoulder. On the way across the field Luke and Eddie took their time and worried about Dan.

"Let me carry him now," Eddie said.

"No, we'll see if he can walk a little," Luke said. It was extraordinary how effectively the old dog could travel on three legs. He hopped along briskly. Sometimes he would stop and let the wounded leg come down firmly, as if testing it, then come hopping along again until Luke picked him up again.

"We should take it easy," Luke said. "We should rest a little now and then." When they got to the road leading to the mill they sat down in the grass and took turns stroking Dan's head.

Going along that road, and resting every three hundred yards, Luke and Eddie conducted a conversation on a high and dignified plane. They were beginning a new relationship with each other. They both knew it and so they were a little shy and very respectful to each other. While they were talking about Dan, they were really trying to draw closer together. Eddie was offering a sincere admiring friendship and Luke knew it and accepted it gravely.

On the road at Mr. Kemp's place Luke said, "I think I'll go in here, Eddie. Mr. Kemp's a friend of mine and he'll look at that slash on Dan's leg. I don't want my uncle to see it."

"That's a good idea, Luke," Eddie said. "Well, I'll look for you this afternoon."

"At the dock. Sure, Eddie."

"Yeah. At the dock. Well I'll be seeing you, Luke."

"Yeah, I'll be seeing you, Eddie."

Halfway up the path Luke suddenly dropped on his knees and put his arms around Dan and whispered, "You're a wonderful old dog, Dan." He couldn't explain why he was so moved and grateful. It was as if the dog had really been struggling not only against the big wild Thor, but against the barrier between Luke and the other boys, and trying to make them truly friendly with Luke. From now on he could be free and happy with them all. "You're some dog, Dan," he whispered, rubbing his face against the dog's nose, trying to show his gratitude.

They found Mr. Kemp out at the barn, and he enjoyed helping them; he got a pail of hot water and bathed Dan's wound and expressed the opinion that Dan would be running around on four legs in a few days. He agreed with Luke that it would be better not to tell Uncle Henry what had happened.

But when he got back to the mill and saw Uncle Henry going toward the house, mounting the veranda steps, opening the screen door, his step decisive, his face so full of sensible determination, Luke longed to be able to tell him what had happened; not only because the dog was Uncle Henry's property, and property ought to be protected, but because he suddenly believed as he glanced at Uncle Henry's burly shoulders that Uncle Henry would have done just what he himself had done, and would be proud of him. "Why, the sensible thing would have been to pick up a club and smack that crazy dog on the head," he could almost hear Uncle Henry say. "Why that's just what I did, Uncle Henry," Luke imagined himself explaining as he followed Uncle Henry into the house. "That was the practical thing, Luke. The only practical thing. That dog was our property," Uncle Henry would agree. "I can certainly see that anything we own around here is going to be well looked after by you, Luke."

But of course he would never be able to see this glow of approval in his uncle's eyes, which was so important to him, because he had promised Elmer that he would not tell Uncle Henry.

13. A Useless Thing

Uncle Henry didn't notice that the dog limped badly for a week, or if he did notice it, he didn't say anything to Luke. The summer holidays had come and on the afternoon of Civic Holiday, Uncle Henry drove Luke and Aunt Helen in to the fair grounds. On that day there were to be trotting races and the judging of livestock and a ball game between the town team and a team from the crew of the *City of Cleveland,* which was in the harbor.

Luke wanted to take Dan in the car with them, but Uncle Henry said that Dan's job was to stay home and watch the place. If he wasn't a watchdog now, what was he, Uncle Henry asked. So Dan followed the car to the highway and then turned back to the house.

At the fair grounds Luke stayed with his aunt and uncle for the first half hour out of politeness, going with them to look at the display of fruit and vegetables, and then to look at the prize cattle and listen to his uncle talking professionally about a powerful Holstein bull, or a champion Jersey milk cow. With a cigar in one hand, the words rolling out of him authoritatively, Uncle Henry was just as impressive talking about cattle as he was about lumber in the mill. He had on a fine, well-pressed, gray suit, and wore a heavy gold watch chain, and looked so impressive that Luke was proud of him. He looked like a big, open-hearted, generous man, and he gave Luke a dollar to spend on ice cream and hot dogs. He knew Luke wanted to get out in the field, for they had erected a merry-go-round, and the ball game was on, and all the kids were out there. The part of the fair that Luke liked, the noise and erratic gaiety and the happy disorder, was the part that Uncle Henry wanted to avoid. Luke could see that Uncle Henry was not at home in a jolly fair grounds or in a circus. Everything was too disorderly and unplanned and careless and it all went against his nature, but he said to Luke, "You can run along by yourself now, Luke, and have some fun, and I'll meet you at five o'clock by the judges' stand after the races are over."

Soon all the kids were together on the third-base line rooting for the home team, which won the game in the ninth when Winkie Purvis hit a triple into the crowd in right field with two men on base. Then came the trotting races, which were run in heats. Some of the fastest horses for miles around were entered in these races. Luke, who had never seen trotting races in the city, was delighted; the town suddenly became a wonderful place to live in.

On the way home they talked cheerfully about the fair.

They were hungry and glad to get home. When the car turned up the road and approached the house, Luke expected to hear Dan bark and come running to the car.

"Where's that old dog?" Uncle Henry asked.

"I guess he's on the veranda," Luke said.

"Looks as if we haven't got a watchdog any more," Uncle Henry said casually.

When they got out of the car there was Dan on the veranda sleeping peacefully.

Aunt Helen bustled around the kitchen with Luke helping her and following her instructions accurately. Working for Aunt Helen in the kitchen was something like working for Uncle Henry in the mill. The little tasks she had assigned to Luke had to be done smoothly and neatly or she lost patience. Her face shone with energetic determination. A big white apron now covered her good flowered chintz dress. In her kitchen she was as dominating a figure as Uncle Henry was in the mill.

Uncle Henry ate an enormous meal, and finally leaned back and took a cigar from his vest pocket. Puffing on his cigar, he ambled out to the veranda where the collie was sleeping. With a sigh he sat down in the rocking chair, put his head back and began to enjoy his cigar. After Luke and Aunt Helen had washed the dishes, they joined Uncle Henry on the veranda. At that time of day, with only a few red streaks of sunlight on the water, it was cool and pleasant. Luke was sitting on the steps, his back against the veranda post; the collie was sleeping behind Uncle Henry's chair; and Aunt Helen, sighing blissfully, had stretched herself out in the hammock. "Well, there's another day," she murmured.

Luke always enjoyed sitting with them on the veranda after dinner. At that hour they all seemed to belong to each other. Not that anything much was said. It was not the time for important conversations. No one expected him to be alert and attentive. It was the hour of twilight peacefulness around the mill when it was considered respectable to be a little lazy and indolent while Uncle Henry was digesting his dinner.

Then Luke, who had been eyeing the sleeping collie, began to tap the veranda with his fingers as if he were a telegrapher tapping out a message. The three long taps, the three short ones were like a signal to Dan. The old collie, lifting his head, got up stiffly, stretched, half shook himself, wagged his tail in a lazy acknowledgment that the signal had been heard, and began to cross the veranda to Luke.

But the sleepy dog had his bad eye to the rocking chair where Uncle Henry, rocking lazily back and forth, made the veranda boards squeak. In passing the chair Dan's left front paw went under the rocker just as it came down. The paw was crushed. With a frantic yelp the dog went bounding down the steps and hobbled around the corner of the house. There he stopped for he heard Luke coming after him. All the dog needed was the touch of Luke's hand; he was soothed; as if apologizing, he began to lick the boy's hand.

"What on earth—" Uncle Henry had cried as he jumped out of the chair. Aunt Helen, too, had been so startled she had nearly fallen out of the hammock.

"Oh my goodness," Aunt Helen said in a scolding tone. "I was dozing. What happened? I got such a start."

"It was nothing," Uncle Henry said, but he was watching Luke and the dog. He, too, had been startled. Now he had the mildly outraged feeling of a man who has jumped in alarm only to find that the noise that scared him was not worth noticing; he was ruffled and indignant. But as he went on watching the dog, he became calm and meditative. For the first time in months the dog had his shrewd and full attention.

"Luke," Uncle Henry called sharply. "Bring that dog here."

When Luke led the dog back to the veranda, Uncle Henry said quietly, "Thanks, Luke." Taking out a cigar he lit it, put his hands on his knees and frowned and eyed the dog steadily. Obviously he was making some kind of an important decision about the collie.

"What's the matter, Uncle Henry?" Luke asked nervously.

"That dog can't see any more," Uncle Henry said.

"Oh, yes he can," Luke said quickly. "His bad eye got turned to the chair, that's all, Uncle Henry."

"Poor old fellow," Uncle Henry went on, scratching his head and frowning. "His eyesight's just about gone. He's through, all right. Just eating and sleeping and getting in the way. The other day I tripped over him on the veranda. Can't even use him for a watchdog now."

"Uncle Henry," Luke said quickly, "you don't want to make a mistake about it. Dan knows everything that goes on around here."

"Yeah," Uncle Henry said, but he wasn't paying much attention to Luke. "Helen," he said, turning to his wife, "sit up a minute, will you?"

"Oh, dear, I was just cooling off, Henry."

"It's about this poor old dog, Helen."

"What about him, Henry?"

"I was thinking about Dan the other day. It's not just that Dan's about blind, but did you notice that when we drove up before dinner he didn't even bark?"

"That's a fact, Henry, he didn't, come to think of it."

"No, not much good even for a watchdog now."

"Uncle Henry," Luke said desperately, "just a minute." As Uncle Henry turned to him idly, Luke went closer to him until he was standing right at the arm of the chair and talking to him as he had never talked before, talking openly and firmly and as if they had a deep respect for each other.

"Dan is a strange old dog, Uncle Henry," he said. "Well, you know what he's like, only maybe you haven't been looking at him the last while as much as I have." Fumbling a little his eyes shifted to his aunt, then back to his uncle's eyes; and because the far-away meditative expression was still in Uncle Henry's eye, Luke wanted to find elegant words that would bring Uncle Henry close to him and make him attentive.

"Dan can lie there on the veranda and know every little thing that's going on, Uncle Henry," he said. "I've found that out. I can pass on the veranda and Dan will seem to be asleep but his eye will flicker open. He'll know it's me by the step, just as he knows your step and Aunt Helen's step, and the step of everybody that belongs around here. It's the same with all kinds of noises, Uncle Henry. He knows what noises belong around this place. And of course he knows the sound of our car. I've found that out. I'll bet you anything, Uncle Henry, that when you drove up today and Dan was sleeping on the veranda, his eye opened and he listened, and when he recognized the sound of our car he knew it was all right and he knew he didn't have to come leaping out. If it was another car, he could have told us about it as soon as he heard the engine on the road. I can tell the sound of our car, and so can Dan. That's why he didn't come out, Uncle Henry."

"Why, that's quite a speech, my boy," Uncle Henry said admiringly.

"Well, it's the truth, Uncle Henry."

"Did you hear Luke, Helen?" Uncle Henry asked. "The boy could make a fine lawyer when he grows up. H-m, h-m," he said, smiling a little.

Growing serious again, he went on, "But even so, Luke," and he made a clucking noise in his throat and glanced again at Dan, "supposing the dog knows the familiar sounds. What good does it do? His eyes are gone, he's slow and lazy, and the plain fact is that his teeth are gone too..."

"Why, those teeth could tear a man to pieces, Uncle Henry."

"H-m. And he's no good for hunting either," Uncle Henry went on. "And he eats a lot, I suppose, Helen?"

"About as much as he ever did, Henry," Aunt Helen said with a shrug. It was the shrug and her tone that frightened

Luke. This conversation was not really important to Aunt Helen. Uncle Henry was at least making a decision but Aunt Helen was hardly concerned. Luke couldn't even bear to look at her, for her plump pink face with the little drops of moisture on her upper lip frightened him even more than Uncle Henry's calmness.

"The plain fact is the old dog isn't worth his keep any more," Uncle Henry said. After a little pause he shrugged and his mind was made up. "Well," he said, "that's that. It's time we got rid of him. Of course you're fond of him, Luke. We are too. We've been mighty good to him. And even now we have to do what's good for him," he explained gently. "We have to do the sensible thing even if we don't like it."

They had heard Luke's plea for the dog; they had heard him offer his judgment; but to them it was a boy's judgment, sentimental, dreamy, childish and inevitable; it was not to have any weight with Uncle Henry when he was solemnly coming to a practical conclusion. Realizing that what he might say wasn't going to have any influence, Luke waited stiffly and their words seemed to pound against his heart.

"It's always hard to know how to get rid of an old dog, Henry," Aunt Helen said with a sigh.

"That's a fact, Helen. I was thinking about it the other day. Some people think it best to shoot a dog. Easier on the dog and so on. Maybe it is. But I haven't had any shells for that shotgun for over a year. Poisoning is a hard death for a dog. I've no use for people who poison their dogs. I certainly wouldn't do it myself. Maybe drowning is the easiest and quickest way. Well, I'll speak to one of the mill hands and have him look after it."

Crouching on the veranda, his arms around the old dog's head, Luke cried out, "Uncle Henry, Dan's a wonderful dog. You don't know how wonderful a dog he is."

"Yes, he's been a fine dog, Luke," Uncle Henry agreed, puffing on the cigar. As Luke watched the blue smoke drifting across the veranda, he wondered why the right words which would explain how wonderful Dan was wouldn't come; he couldn't even find any words; he only felt bewildered. All the ways in which Dan was wonderful he had felt many times, but now it was all only a feeling which could not be explained persuasively.

"You see, my boy," Uncle Henry went on in a kindly tone, "I know you like Dan, and we've always liked Dan, too. The time comes when you have to get rid of any old dog no matter how much you like him. Surely you have the sense to see that, Luke. We've got to be practical about it. It's best for the dog. Dan's had a long life and a good easy one and now he's in the way. He doesn't earn his keep and he has to be fed. What else is there to do?"

"Let him stay around, Uncle Henry—please."

"With a horse or a dog, Luke, there comes a time when you have to do the sensible thing. You have to be practical. It isn't that I don't want a dog around here. We should have a dog around here. One that will be useful and worth his keep. So I'll get you a pup, my boy. A fine smart little dog that will become useful. A pup that will grow up with you, Luke."

"I don't want a pup," Luke cried, turning his face away. He didn't want Uncle Henry to see the tears in his eyes. If Uncle Henry saw the tears, it would ónly convince him that Luke was very young and inclined to be unpractical; he would be all the more firmly convinced that Luke needed instruction in good hard common sense.

Circling around, the dog began to bark, then flick his tongue at the back of Luke's neck to show him he understood that he was unhappy.

On the veranda there was a long silence, and the twilight deepened, and up the road from Mr. Kemp's place came the moo of a cow, then the silence again, and then from behind the woods the lonely cry of a freight train. The shadows of the bush had fallen across the river, which was a deep olive green now.

Catching her husband's eye, Aunt Helen put her fingers warningly to her lips. It was foolish to go on talking in front of the boy. Being a kindly woman she felt sorry for Luke; but she believed he was sensible enough to be concerned not only with what was best for the dog but what in the long run would be best for Luke, too. No one liked to see a faithful old dog disposed of; but on the other hand there was an end on earth to the life of every living thing; Uncle Henry knew better than anybody when a life was no longer useful. A boy's emotions were changeable. What seemed unbearably sorrowful at one moment could be forgotten two days later. And all that was needed, she believed, was a little tact.

"An old dog like Dan gets a feeling in his bones that his days are over," she said lightly. "The time and the season.

You know what I mean, don't you, Henry, and I think Dan has had that feeling for some time."

"Oh, sure," Uncle Henry agreed.

"An old dog like Dan often disappears quietly," she said. "They often wander off into the brush and pick a place to die when the time comes. Isn't that so, Henry?" she asked pointedly.

"Oh, sure," he agreed again. "In fact when Dan didn't show up yesterday, I was sure that was what had happened to him. In fact that's probably what will happen to him. So we don't have to worry about how to dispose of him. Forget it, Luke," he said, and he yawned, and seemed to forget about the dog himself.

But Luke knew his uncle did not reach a practical decision after a lot of pondering and then idly forget about it. To Uncle Henry a decision arrived at was as good as an action taken. Uncle Henry had no use for men who knew what should be done and weakly avoided action for sentimental reasons. So Luke was frightened. If Uncle Henry had decided to dispose of the collie, he would be ashamed of himself if he were diverted by a boy's affection for him.

"Well, I think I'll take a little walk," Luke said self-consciously.

"It's getting dark, Luke. Don't go away," Aunt Helen said. "It feels a little like rain to me."

"No, it's not going to rain," Uncle Henry said firmly.

"I'll just be down by the river," Luke said. As he started down the path, Dan got up and followed him.

At the river's edge he sat on a rock, his hand on the dog's

head, staring across at the great tree shadows which were closing over the river and closing over him. A few stars were out. Beyond the mouth of the river was the smooth glowing line of the lake. In that light the lake always glowed; and when the darkness deepened the glowing line faded into the horizon, and when the moon came out there was the long glowing ladder of moonlight. His heart seemed to be jerking painfully. Though he tried to think he was aware of nothing but the jerking thump against his ribs.

"Come on, Dan," he said, and he followed the river right down to the mouth and went along the beach a hundred yards. It was dark now and the moon was suddenly obscured by a mass of heavy clouds. A breeze came up. Standing on the beach with the dog beside him, he stared into the blackness of the lake. A wind ruffled the water. The wind came sudden and strong, blowing his pants against his legs, blowing his hair back, and the dog, his fur ruffled in the wind, looked up at him, mystified by his silence and the way he was staring across the darkening lake. Sometimes Dan would look out there, too, as if trying to see what held Luke's attention.

"You know something, Dan," Luke said, "it may rain after all." The sound of his own voice talking to the dog broke his strange inert loneliness. He suddenly longed to be able to think clearly. If he could fight for Dan as he had been willing to fight the big dog, Thor, it would be easy; he could win. But he couldn't hit Uncle Henry on the head as he had hit Thor. He couldn't struggle with Uncle Henry because Dan belonged to Uncle Henry. Not only was Uncle

Henry Dan's owner, he was also the guardian and owner of him, Luke. They both belonged to Uncle Henry, who was the final implacable authority in their lives and a man who never yielded authority.

In his heart Luke knew that he couldn't move his uncle. All he could do, he thought, was to keep the dog away from him, keep him out of the house, feed him when Uncle Henry wasn't around.

"Come on, Dan," he said. "I don't want them looking for us, or calling us, or noticing us at all," and he led the way back to the house and through the living room where his aunt and his uncle were reading peacefully, and up to his own room.

When he had got undressed he sat on the bed with Dan and tried to tell himself that if Uncle Henry didn't notice the collie for a few days he might forget about him, especially if he were very busy at the mill. After all, the collie was utterly unimportant in Uncle Henry's life. Months ago he had intended to get rid of the collie and had kept putting it off.

It started to rain, and there was a flash of lightning across the lake. The wind rose and the waves began to roll on the shore. The wind blew through the open window. The rain began to drum on the roof. "Uncle Henry was wrong," he thought. "It did rain." It was a hopeful sign. Finally Luke lay back on the bed, and before he fell asleep with his arm around Dan's neck, he remembered his uncle's face as he sniffed the smell of the fresh wood and said, "Ah, that's a delightful smell," and that also was a hopeful sign.

14. Where the River Was Deep

IN the morning, the shaft of bright sunlight across Luke's face woke him and he sat up quickly, calling, "Dan." When he heard the scraping and stirring on the floor at the end of the bed, he relaxed in relief. "I just wondered, that's all, Dan," he whispered.

Having dressed, he hurried downstairs, let the dog out and returned to have breakfast with his aunt and uncle. And it seemed like any other breakfast on any other morning, with Uncle Henry being jolly and friendly and Aunt Helen insisting that Luke eat heartily. Usually Luke squirmed a little when she pressed him to eat; now it seemed that what happened to him was very important to her. That was what he wanted. He wanted to believe they were concerned about his health and his happiness and about anything that might trouble him.

And Uncle Henry hadn't even looked up when Luke was letting the dog out. This seemed to indicate that he had forgotten about the collie.

"It rained, didn't it, Uncle Henry?" Luke said quietly.

"Why, yes, it did, Luke."

"Don't you remember you said it wasn't going to rain?" Luke said, as if he were reminding Uncle Henry that it was possible for him to be wrong in his judgment.

"Yes," Uncle Henry said with a smile. "And in spite of my opinion that it wouldn't rain. However, a rain like that will do the crops around here a lot of good. It's what the fields need. A very useful rain."

Though the rainfall had come in violation of Uncle Henry's judgment of the weather, he accepted the violation cheerfully because the rain was needed.

"What are you going to do this morning, Luke?" he asked cheerfully.

"I don't know...yet," Luke said cautiously.

"I was wondering if you'd like to go along the shore and pick me some raspberries in that good patch before the neighbors clean it out entirely," Aunt Helen said.

"Well, I could. Yes, I guess I could."

"Look, Luke," Uncle Henry said seriously. "You be businesslike about it. People pick berries to sell them. You strike a bargain first with your aunt."

"A box of berries would cost me about twenty cents," Aunt Helen said. "Although if they're a little mashed and turning, I sometimes get them for ten and I can do them down as well as the good ones. What's your offer, Luke?"

"What'll you give me?" he asked, with not much enthusiasm for he was watching their faces suspiciously, wondering why they were getting him out of the way.

"I'll give you ten cents a box."

"Okay," he said. "I'll get to it." Then he added firmly, "I'll take Dan with me."

The sun was strong and it would be hot in the berry patch, so he took an old straw hat and he got a pail from the kitchen. He deliberately took a lot of time so he would be going out of the house at the same time Uncle Henry was crossing over to the sawmill. They went out together. Luke then whistled for the dog, his heart thumping a little as he waited to see if Uncle Henry would say, "Don't bother taking the dog with you, Luke."

Dan came trotting around the side of the house and Uncle Henry didn't even notice him. "If I were you I'd pick berries every morning, Luke," he said earnestly. "If you can't sell them to your aunt, you can sell them anywhere along the line, and there's nothing like the feel of money that you earn yourself. Well, so long, Luke. Remember, you're in business now."

"So long, Uncle Henry," Luke said and he watched his uncle go along the path with his big important stride, his white shirt spotless in the morning sunlight, the small straw hat on the back of his head.

"You know something, Dan," Luke said as they went down to the river to get in the boat. "Uncle Henry is a reasonable man. A very reasonable man. I certainly talked to him last night, and maybe he liked the way I talked, and now he's had a chance to think over what I said about you. If it made sense, why, he'd be the first one to see it."

He was really only offering encouragement to himself. He still couldn't quite believe that anything he could say would sound wise and persuasive enough to alter Uncle Henry's judgment. The main thing was that Dan was still with him.

Usually when they got into the boat, they played their game and the dog became Captain Dan and they had their splendid conversations and the river and the woods and the whole world changed. And wanting it to be like any other morning, Luke cried out, "Here we are, Captain Dan!" But he couldn't go on with it. It sounded feeble. His own mind wouldn't leap to the fantasy. Even the words 'Captain Dan' worried him. The real world was now too painfully close to him, and too sharp and hard. So he rowed slowly and watched the bugs on the water. With his head on one side, the collie watched him and wondered. Once he let out an encouraging bark, as if to say, "We usually have a lot of quick fine conversation right here, don't we, Luke?"

Beaching the boat, they went down the beach as far as the spot where the kids played tree tag on the vines. Luke was glad he had worn the old straw hat for the sun was strong. In no time the handle of the pail began to burn; the water on the lake sparkled so brightly he couldn't even see the blue line where the drop began. In the woods it was sheltered from the sun, and yet actually hotter because the trees shut out the cool little breeze from the lake.

No one else was at the berry patch—it was too early—and Luke was glad, for he didn't want to talk to anybody. It was as if he had to think calmly and seriously while he worked. Yet when the dog lay down in a cool spot by a rock and Luke got into the berry patch he was really working rapidly so he wouldn't have to think. All that mattered was that he should get a big pail of fine fresh raspberries so his aunt would feel happy. It was important that everybody should feel happy. While they were all feeling happy and satisfied, no one would want to do anything to break the happiness.

His back got tired, the pail got heavy, and the sun was directly overhead. He lay down and rested a while. "We'd better get right back to the house, Dan, while Uncle Henry is having his lunch," he said. "Maybe when he sees all these berries... Well, you know how much Uncle Henry admires an industrious man. Come on."

Going along the beach in the hot sun, carrying the heavy pail of berries, the hat that was too big for him slipping down over his eyes and making his head sweat, was a wearying journey. Dan just loafed along till they got to the river, then he bounded ahead, jumped eagerly into the boat and waited expectantly.

At the sawmill it was quiet. The saws had stopped screeching. No one was moving around in the hot noon hour. After he had pulled the boat up at the little dock, Luke said to Dan, "Don't you come with me, Dan. Go on. Go on around to the back of the house. Go on. You see, maybe if you keep out of sight, you can pass right out of Uncle Henry's mind."

Blinking at him with a mournful expression in its amber eye, the old dog stayed there; and Luke, gripping the pail in both hands, staggered toward the house.

"My goodness, look at all the berries that boy picked," Aunt Helen cried enthusiastically, as Luke staggered in. "Just look for yourself, Henry. There's a boy for you. There's a berry picker."

Uncle Henry, who had just finished his lunch, wiped his mouth with his napkin and beamed his approval. "No one will ever call that boy lazy," he said warmly.

These were fine words and they delighted Luke. He wanted them to approve of him. As he sat down, wiped his forehead and took the glass of cold milk his aunt handed him, he said, "Aw, I'm not tired. I'm not even really hungry." Tired as he was, he swung his leg indolently as if he were only waiting for them to ask him to do something else for them.

"Don't just hand the berries to your aunt, Luke. Have her measure them out right now," Uncle Henry insisted. "And see that you check the measurement. Be exact. It's ten cents a box. You did all right there, Luke," he said, and he went out on his way back to the mill.

While Aunt Helen was measuring out the berries, Luke had gone to the screen door to watch his uncle. It was as if he had to be aware of every move Uncle Henry made so he could understand what was in his mind. Both his hands were pressed against the screen door, and his eyes were alert.

Dan was nowhere to be seen. That was good; it was important that Uncle Henry should not have a picture of the dog in his mind as he went into the mill.

Then Uncle Henry, who was approaching the entrance of the mill, suddenly stopped and called out to old Sam Carter, who had gone into the mill ahead of him. Sam Carter turned back and they stood there together, with Uncle Henry doing most of the talking and Sam Carter nodding and understanding. Even at that it was a familiar picture. It was all right. Uncle Henry often stood talking to Sam and Sam always listened patiently and attentively. But then a little thing happened. Uncle Henry suddenly took a cigar from his vest pocket and gave it to Sam Carter.

Luke had never seen his uncle give Sam Carter a cigar. Uncle Henry would never hand a cigar to one of his working men on the job just as a friendly gesture.

While Luke was eating his lunch all he could think of was this picture of Sam Carter reaching for the cigar and nodding his head understandingly.

And when Luke had finished his lunch and was out on the veranda, Uncle Henry, coming toward the house, called, "Luke, come here, will you?"

"Yes, Uncle Henry," Luke said.

"I'm out of cigars, my boy. Should have got a supply yesterday at the drug store. Nothing seems to go right unless I have a cigar in my mouth."

It was true that he always had a cigar in his mouth when he was in the mill, though he sometimes forgot to light it.

"I want you to hop on your bike, Luke, and go into town and get me some cigars. Here's the money."

"Sure. I might as well take Dan with me," Luke said.

"Better not, son," Uncle Henry said. "It'll take you all afternoon. I need a cigar."

"Dan can keep up with me, Uncle Henry."

"Luke, you ought to know it's too hot a day to run a dog that far and back, trailing you on your bike. I want those cigars in a hurry, Luke."

"Okay," Luke said.

"That's the boy. Get going, Luke," Uncle Henry said. His uncle's tone was so casual that Luke could hardly believe they were merely trying to get rid of him. Anyway, he had to do what he was told. He had never dared to refuse to obey his uncle's order. But when he had taken his bicycle and had ridden down the path that followed the stream to the town road, and had got about a quarter of a mile along the road, he found that all he could think of was that picture of his uncle handing the cigar to Sam Carter.

Sick with worry he got off the bike and stood uncertainly on the hot, sunlit, dusty, gravel road. Ahead a long swirling cloud of dust from a car drifted to the left and settled over the fields. Luke remained motionless, looking beyond the town at the blue mountains which had always beckoned and stirred him so mysteriously, and as he contemplated their blueness he seemed to be waiting for some portent. On a clear day like this the veil of mist which usually hung over the mountains was lifted and they became starkly blue. His eyes wandered helplessly to the sky over the lake where a patch of round full clouds were shaping themselves into a white castle over the blue water.

Sam Carter, he thought, was a gruff, aloof old man who would have no feeling for a dog. Sam Carter, a man who dragged himself dumbly through life knowing only one rule of conduct, which was to do exactly what Uncle Henry told him to do, was the one who had kicked at the dog the first day Luke had come to the mill. Of all the men at the mill, Sam Carter would surely be the one Uncle Henry would ask to destroy a dog.

Suddenly Luke could go no further without getting some assurance that the dog would not be harmed while he was away.

From that spot on the road he could look across the field at an angle and see the house behind the rim of tree and the smoke coming from the chimney. If he could get close enough to the house so Dan could hear him, he could whistle softly; if Dan came running to him, he would know then that Uncle Henry's conversation with Sam Carter had had nothing to do with the dog; his mind would be at peace, and he would let the collie follow him along the road about a quarter of a mile and then tell him to wait by the big tree stump where he usually waited after school; then he could hurry on to town.

Leaving the bike in the ditch, he started to cross the field; he was trying to keep out of the range of the house windows. In this field the grass was tall and there was a lot of sweet-smelling clover in bud, almost up to his waist.

About fifty yards away from the house he whistled softly, and waited. But there was no sign of the dog who, of course, might be asleep at the front of the house or over behind the sawmill in the shady spot by the river. When the saws whined, a dog couldn't hear a soft whistle, so he whistled louder; he did not dare to whistle like that again. For a few minutes he couldn't make up his mind what to do. Finally he decided to go back to the road, get on his bike, go back to where the river path joined the road, and leave his bike there and go through the tall grass to the front of the house and the sawmill without being seen.

Back at the road and on his bike again, he prepared a story which would justify his return if his aunt should happen to see him. Any little story about his bike would do; the back tire could need a little air; if the tire were soft and he came back to blow it up, Uncle Henry would commend him for it. It would look as if he were a sensible boy concerned about the care of his expensive bike.

At the river path he dismounted, let a little air out of the back tire, and left the bike there; if he were seen, he could pretend he was on his way to get the bicycle pump. He followed the river path for about a hundred yards. When he came to the place where the river began to bend sharply toward the house, his heart fluttered and his legs felt paralyzed, for there he saw the old rowboat in the place where the river was deep and in the rowboat was Sam Carter with the collie.

15. The Practical Proposition

THE bearded man in the blue overalls was contentedly smoking the cigar Uncle Henry had given him; the dog with a rope around his neck sat quietly beside him, his tongue sometimes going out in a tentative friendly lick at the brown hand holding the rope.

It was all like a crazy dream picture; all wrong because it looked so lazy and friendly; even the curling smoke from Sam Carter's cigar looked companionable. And the boat was there in a shaded spot on the river where the water was shadowed olive green. In the trees a woodpecker noisily drilled at a tree. The first wisp of blue smoke from the cigar had softly risen and had drifted ten feet away from the boat. Sam Carter seemed to be hardly aware of the dog's presence in the boat; the moment had little importance for him.

Holding the cigar out in his hand, he inspected it with satis-faction, then sniffed at it as if he were calculating what it had cost Uncle Henry.

Sam Carter's left hand hanging deep in the water held a foot of rope with a heavy stone at the end. Flicking the ashes from the end of the cigar, Sam thrust it into his mouth, as if he were ready for action. Until Sam made this decisive gesture, Luke seemed to have been hynotized by the peaceful calmness of the scene. But when Sam dropped the heavy stone, Luke cried out wildly, "Don't, please don't!"—But the cry was drowned by the shriek of the saws at the mill. Even so Dan's head had jerked up in recognition of that cry which had come too late. As the collie jumped at the water, half pulled there anyway by the tightening rope around his neck, he went into a long shallow dive except that the hind legs suddenly kicked up above the water, and then shot down; and Luke watching it sobbed and trembled, for it was as though the happy secret part of his life around the sawmill was vanishing forever.

But even as he watched, mute and helpless, he seemed to be following a plan without knowing it; he was already fumbling in his pocket for his jackknife. Jerking the blade open he pulled off his pants, kicked off his shoes, and prayed that Sam Carter would quickly get out of sight.

Carter, who had watched the spot on the water where the dog had disappeared until it was smooth and unbroken by any little ripple or bubble, now looked vaguely at the river bank as if wondering if he had heard a cry come from there. He searched the brushes and the grass. He squinted and pondered. A stupid expression came on his face. Then he began to row slowly to the bank, pointing the boat toward a spot about twenty feet farther up from the place where Luke lay hidden.

All Sam Carter's movements were so slow and deliberate that Luke prayed, "Oh, make him hurry, God. Oh, please, please, please, why doesn't he hurry?" Inside himself he was tightened up like a spring. He edged a little closer to the water; his legs trembled, his body struggled against the strange power in his mind that held him back cautiously and forced him to wait. If he dashed out into the water now, Sam would see him and block the way. Sam Carter, having been given definite instructions to drown the dog, would carry out those instructions, Luke knew, even if he had to keep the boat over the spot in the water where Dan had gone down for the last time. While he was holding on to himself, Luke could not take his eyes off that one spot in the water.

Sam Carter, rowing lazily to the river bank, stepped out of the boat, and in his dull methodical fashion he began to draw the boat up on the bank. It took him about two minutes to do this. Luke kept whispering, "Dan's in the water. Dan's dying. Dan's choking to death." Though his lips hardly moved, it was like a desperate shrieking protest, loud and terrifying in the darkness of his own mind. It was so hard holding on to himself that he started to sob again, and the river, the boat, the trees and the sky blurring before his eyes seemed to lurch and become black; he felt dizzy and thought he was going to faint. But the one part of his mind which was quick and wonderfully clear was calculating that Dan could stay two minutes under water unless he was choking to death. A person could be dragged from the water after being under three minutes or even five. "Oh, Dan, Dan," he whispered and it was like an agonized apology.

Sam Carter, having hauled the boat up on the bank, took the cigar out of his mouth and spat at the water. Then he took a red bandana handkerchief from his hip pocket and wiped his mouth carefully. He blew his nose loudly. Putting the handkerchief back in his pocket, he looked in the direction of the sawmill; he even took a step in that direction, then remembered that he was smoking the cigar, and he couldn't go into the mill with the lighted cigar in his mouth. The boss mightn't like it. Only the boss smoked cigars on the job. Sam rarely had a chance to smoke during working hours. A fragrant cigar, once it had been put out, never tasted as good when lighted again. So Sam took a deep puff, exhaled slowly with vast satisfaction, then turned and sat down on the boat to snatch a few moments of pleasure with the cigar.

When he saw Sam Carter sit down on the boat and cross his legs comfortably, Luke felt such a heaviness in his heart that he wanted to moan. As if he were very close to the dog in the water, so close he could whisper to him or make him feel his thoughts, Luke kept repeating desperately, "Just a few seconds more, Dan. A little more. It can still be all right." He was trying to measure the seconds by the beating of his own heart. It seemed to be important to the collie that he should keep on counting, "One, two, three, four, five, six, seven, eight, nine, ten." But the seconds, as measured by his heartbeats, came very slowly and when his heart did thud, it was so loud and painful and so high in his throat that it frightened him. He couldn't bear to go on dragging the moments out by recognizing and counting each one. "I'll give him ten seconds more," he thought. "If he doesn't go then, I've got to jump in." But the ten seconds were too hard to count; he couldn't bear to go on with a count that seemed to be measuring what was left of Dan's life. Crouching on his bare knees, a pebble under the right knee bruising it, a twig sticking into the left knee, the palms of his hands flat on the ground, he peered through the brush at Sam Carter.

The delicate white ash at the end of the cigar got a little heavier; it was an inch long; and Sam was looking at it as if he understood that a seasoned smoker of fine cigars never knocked the ash off until the last moment; even a fine tobacco leaf would not burn evenly if the ash were removed too cleanly. The removal of the ash was to be a neat, calculated little operation. The slow, dull, weary man was having his little stolen sensual moment with the good cigar.

Then Sam Carter turned slowly and his eyes narrowed and he listened, his bearded face full of suspicion, for Luke had made a little sound as he shifted his weight from one knee to the other. A twig had cracked. It was as if Sam Carter sensed that he was being watched, and if he were being watched, it meant that he was being rebuked for loafing on the job, and such a rebuke would be unfair and intolerable, for Sam Carter never loafed around the sawmill. With an apprehensive, guilty, self-conscious air he stood up, puffing the cigar rapidly and making thick blue smoke. He began to stroll up the river, his heavy work boots scraping on pebbles and twigs.

"Not just yet, not just yet," Luke thought as his heart jumped, for he was trembling with eagerness to leap at the water. Sam Carter was slinking furtively around the bend as if he felt that he was being observed, but the slosh, slosh, slosh of his boots could still be heard.

As the sounds faded Luke was watching raptly the spot on the water where Dan had disappeared, and just as if he were a keyed-up sprinter waiting for the moment to break, cried out within himself, "Now!" Sliding down the bank, he took a wild-eyed leap at the water, the sun glistening on his slender body as he splashed out to the deep place. He arched his back and dived, swimming under water, his open eyes getting used to the greenish haze. He held the jack-knife in his right hand.

Through the green haze of the water he could see the sandy bottom and some embedded rocks; but it was hard to see clearly for there were lines of light and dark from tree shadows. He was looking for the one line—the rope attached to Dan's body. Then it flashed in his mind that Dan would be lying there on the bottom like a rock or log, heavy and still, and he wouldn't know which was Dan and which was the log or the rock. In a panic now he scraped with his fingers at the first dark object he saw and swung his arm around groping for the rope. But it was only a rock jutting up from the mud. His lungs were swelling painfully; he seemed to be suffocating, and letting himself shoot up to the surface, he sucked in some air, tried desperately to get an accurate bearing from a familiar tree at the point on the river bank where he had been, then dived again. All his strength came back, for the new dive meant new hope. Again he scraped at dark objects, a log, a rock, until that blank dark moment of terror came when there were singing noises in his head and his chest was hurting, and within himself he cried out for help—he cried out to his dead father, "Oh, Dad, Dad," as if his father were beside him.

The pain in his chest was so heavy he could hardly bear it; yet he could still think; he remembered that the current would probably sweep Dan down from the spot where he had gone into the water; a falling stone might even be dragged at an angle through the water. He shot up to the surface, sucked in air and dove again, swimming underwater with the stream for five yards. Then he saw it; he saw it there in the green watery haze. It was motionless and shadowy against the greenish light. He had enough strength to claw his way toward it. With his left hand he reached out and touched it, the fingers sinking into the wet fur.

He was so excited that he could hardly keep himself under water and work effectively. From the collie's neck the rope stretched to the now imbedded rock, and when he grabbed the rope and tried to slash it with one swift cut there seemed to be no strength in his arm; the rope seemed to slide away from him. Again he slashed and the knife came drifting feebly at the rope, bending it as if the knife and the rope were made of rubber. He knew he couldn't stand it any more, not if the rope only bent like that again; he couldn't stand it because his own strength was failing and he knew that each passing second took what was left of Dan's life. Wrapping his legs around the rope, and with his left hand to hold it, the heavy shadow of the dog sinking slowly into the water beside him, he began to saw at threads of the rope, hacking away as the strands parted and flowered out in the water until the last strand snapped. Again he let himself shoot up in the water, and as he sobbed for breath, his mouth wide open, the dog came drifting up slowly, like a water-soaked log. Even as he sucked in the air, Luke was treading water and pulling the collie toward him. And then after fifteen rapid strokes he was away from the deep place and heading across the river. His feet touched bottom.

Hoisting the collie out of the water, he slung him on his shoulder and scrambled toward the bank, lurching and stumbling, for he had no strength left and the collie was like a dead weight.

He staggered up the bank and through the brush and among the trees to a little grass-covered clearing twenty paces from the river, where he fell flat, hugging the dog and trying to warm him with his own body. The touch of the wet cold fur frightened him; for no matter how hard he pressed the dog against him he felt no warmth, no heartbeat, the collie didn't stir, the good amber eye remained closed. "Oh, Dan, Dan," he wailed, and he sat up and looked around helplessly. Then suddenly he wanted to act like a resourceful competent man who couldn't be flustered, and who could do all that could be done for the collie. On his knees now, he stretched the dog out on his belly, drew him down between his own knees, felt with trembling hands for the soft places on the flanks just above the hip bones, and rocked back and forth, pressing with all his might, then relaxing the pressure as he straightened up. He hoped that he was working the dog's lungs like bellows. He had read that many men who had been taken from the water when they seemed to be drowned had been saved in this way.

"Come on, Dan. Come on, old boy," he pleaded softly. "I won't let you die, Dan. I just won't let you. I won't leave you. You've got to be here with me." All that he had ever read, all that he remembered about efforts to save the drowned came back to him, and the parts that he remembered were those instructions that made him fiercely hopeful. "You shouldn't give up for at least an hour," a voice seemed to say. "It's a mistake to quit too soon. Sometimes a man can be under water for half an hour and still be saved. A lot of water is taken into the stomach. But the larynx tends to close and block the passage of the water into the lungs. So don't give up. Keep at it for at least an hour."

As far as he could figure out, the collie had been under water for about five minutes. It had seemed like an hour, or like the large part of a long day, especially when he had been watching Sam Carter; but now as he worked his hands like a bellows he was checking on those movements of

Carter's, and he knew that everything could have happened within six or seven minutes.

"You can do it, Dan. Come on, old boy," he pleaded softly, but the way the head lay on the ground scared him. He kept watching the jaw and the closed mouth which seemed to be like the mouth of a dead dog he had once seen lying on the side of the road. While this picture of the dead dog grew large and hideous in his mind, a little water suddenly trickled from Dan's mouth, and with his heart jumping Luke muttered over and over, "There, see, Dan, it's working, so you can't be dead. Come on, old boy. Why, you can do it, Dan."

Rocking back and forth tirelessly, he went on applying the finger pressure to the flanks till a little more water dribbled from the mouth. Now he was afraid his trembling hands would get out of control and he would break the even rhythm of the pressure. In the collie's body he felt a faint tremor, like a very faint pulsation, a kind of contraction under his fingers. As soon as he felt it he believed that he must have deceived himself, and then it came again. "Oh, Dan," he whispered gratefully. "You're alive. Oh, Dan."

With a sudden cough the collie jerked his head; then came another spluttering cough, the amber eye opened, and they were looking at each other. For a long silent moment they looked at each other steadily. The amber eye didn't even blink. It was a very strange moment of recognition.

Then the collie, thrusting his leg out stiffly, tried to hoist himself up, staggered, tried again, stood there in a stupor, then sat down slowly.

"Take it easy, take it easy, pal," Luke whispered. For a while the dog remained quiet, his flanks trembling, his tongue hanging out while Luke stroked its head gently.

After resting like this for a few minutes, the collie shook his head stubbornly and staggered to his feet again. This time he stood still, the feet planted firmly on the ground, the head down as if making sure where he was and then not believing, for he turned his head and looked back toward the river. It was odd the way he kept on looking back at the river.

Suddenly Dan shook himself like any other wet dog and the splendid spray splashed over Luke's white eager face. Then Dan turned, eyed Luke, and the red tongue came out in a weak grateful lick at Luke's cheek.

"Okay, okay, I know how you feel, Dan. Only now you ought to lie down for a while," Luke whispered, and as the dog lay down beside him Luke closed his eyes, buried his head in the wet flank and wondered why all the muscles of his arms and legs began to jerk in a nervous reaction. "Please stay there, Dan," he said with a deep sigh. "I don't know what's the matter with me now. I just can't move."

Soon he felt strong again and as his thoughts cleared he lay there trying to make a plan. All that was really important, he decided, was to get Dan far away from the house and hidden in some spot where nobody at the house could see him. In some spot in the woods he could tie up Dan and leave him, and go back to the house and get food for him. Luke believed he was thinking very clearly. He wanted to be cunning and resourceful. If he crossed the river again and got his bike and then went into town and purchased the cigars for Uncle Henry and returned to the house, both Aunt Helen and Uncle Henry would pretend they didn't know what had happened to the dog and Aunt Helen would say, "Well, I told you, Luke. An old dog like that will wander off the place when his time has come," and Uncle Henry would agree, "Yes, the dog knew his days were numbered."

Ah, it would be fine to hear them talking like that; he would grin to himself, and later on go into the woods and get Dan and return and say, "What do you know? I found Dan in the woods—just like you said," and how could they protest? He would be tricking them as they had planned to trick him. What a resourceful cunning plan it was, he thought. Naked though he was, he got up and said, "Come on, Dan," and he began to lead the way slowly through the woods. Every few paces they took, the dog stopped to shake the water from his fur. Luke wanted to get to the clearing with the big white stone where he had so often gone with Dan and which now seemed like a sacred protected grove.

But as he made his way delicately over the broken boughs and the twigs and the embedded stones, his feet began to hurt him painfully. One sharp jutting stone hidden beneath fallen leaves cut his left foot, which began to bleed. Low branches from the spruce trees scratched his body. Black flies began to bite his shoulders.

As the way became more painful, his cunning plan seemed to lose its power over him. It began to collapse. It didn't make sense. He wondered how he had been able to persuade himself it could be successful. His clothes were back on the river bank on the other side very near the path, and a workman going down the path, or his uncle looking for him, could see those clothes and realize at once that he had intervened to save the dog. Everybody would know exactly what had happened. The main thing was to get those clothes before anyone saw them. He began to make his way back quickly.

Even if he had got to the big stone, he told himself, and had tied up Dan, it would have been no good. Dan might have howled in the night, or if he got loose he would certainly come home. Sooner or later Uncle Henry would become aware that he had been thwarted; then he would order Sam Carter to shoot the dog.

Back at the river Luke stepped quickly into the water to cool his bleeding feet. "Come on, Dan," he coaxed. At first the collie shied away from the water, and it was only when Luke started to wade out that the dog reluctantly followed, swimming jerkily, with Luke keeping close beside him; when he was swimming himself, Luke still kept within a foot of the collie.

On reaching the other bank Luke ducked, then darted across the path to the tall grass twenty feet farther away, and there he lay flat on his back. "Lie down, Dan," he whispered, and he listened. No one could have seen him. "Stay there, boy," he said. Crawling back through the grass he picked up his clothes and came back to the dog, which was watching him with great curiosity, as if they were once again playing one of their familiar adventurous games.

When he had put on his clothes, Luke said, "I think we'd better get away from this spot, Dan. Keep down, boy. Come on," and he crawled on through the tall grass till they were about seventy-five yards from the place where he had undressed and there they lay down together.

In a little while he heard his aunt calling, "Luke. Where are you, Luke? Come here, Luke."

"Quiet, Dan," Luke whispered.

A few minutes passed and then Uncle Henry called, "Luke, Luke," and he began to come down the path. They could see him standing there, massive and imposing, his hands on his hips, as he looked down the path, a frown on his face, then he turned and went back to the house.

As he watched the sunlight shine on the back of his uncle's neck, the sudden exultation Luke had felt at knowing the collie was safe beside him turned to despair, for he realized that even if he should be forgiven for saving the collie when he saw him drowning, the fact still was that Uncle Henry was not a man to be thwarted. And the more he was thwarted the more unshaken would be his purpose. Uncle Henry had made up his mind to get rid of Dan; in a few days time, in another way, he would get rid of him as he got rid of everything around the mill that he believed to be useless.

Lying there, looking up at the hardly moving clouds, Luke grew more bewildered. He couldn't go back to the house without the collie, nor could the collie be allowed to go anywhere without him. Wherever they went they had to go together.

"I guess there's just no place to go, Dan," he whispered forlornly. "Even if we start off down the road somebody is sure to see us and tell Uncle Henry, then he would come after me and bring me back even if we went to another town, and you'd have to come back with me and then we'd be finished."

All the world's misery seemed to engulf him as he lay there, pondering and concentrating until his head ached, yet unable to make a plan that would overcome and block his uncle's plan. Dan was watching a butterfly circling crazily above them, watching with a twitching nose as he became interested and playful, following the butterfly with his good eye. The collie felt secure because he was with Luke.

Raising himself a little, Luke looked first through the grass at the corner of the house, then he turned and looked the other way to the wide blue lake. A grain boat made a little speck against the skyline and a faint wisp of smoke trailed far behind the speck. The blueness of the lake and the distant ship and the wisp of smoke only deepened Luke's dejection. With a sigh he lay down again, and for hours they lay there until the sounds from the sawmill suddenly ceased and voices could be heard in broken little bits of conversation as the men quit work. Finally two of them came down the path together, then a third, and then came Sam Carter in a slow sluggish stride as if nothing important had happened. The sun moved low in the western sky.

"Well, we can't stay here any longer, Dan," Luke said at last, and he sounded tired. "We'll just have to get as far away as we can. Come on, and keep down, old boy." He began to crawl wearily through the grass, going farther away from the house. When he could no longer be seen, he got up and began to trot across the field to the gravel road leading to town.

On the road the collie would turn anxiously as if wondering why Luke shuffled along, dragging his feet wearily. "I guess you can't quite figure out what's bothering me, eh, Dan? Well, I'm stumped, that's all," Luke explained. "I can't seem to think of a safe place to take you."

Now they were opposite the Kemp place and there was the gate where they had so often turned in together to have their wild game with the cows. And there on the veranda was old Mr. Kemp in the rocking chair, smoking his pipe and enjoying the cool after-dinner breeze from the lake. Suddenly Luke stopped. All he could think of at first was that old Mr. Kemp had liked both him and Dan and had liked watching them playing and was aware of the happiness a boy found in a dog's companionship. Some of the things that weren't valuable to Uncle Henry had a strange value to Mr. Kemp, who seemed able to protect these things that were valuable to him alone. But more important than anything else, Mr. Kemp had been kind and sympathetic; in his own way he seemed to share Luke's secret happiness, and for that reason it had been such a pleasure to help him get the cows in the evening.

Staring at the figure of the old man on the veranda, Luke said to Dan, "If only I could be sure of him, Dan. I know he likes us, but he's a very smart man and he knows you are

Uncle Henry's property and that Uncle Henry is entitled to get rid of you if he wants to. He wouldn't quarrel with Uncle Henry about a thing like this. I know they have a lot of respect for each other, although I don't see how they do it. I guess it's because they're both smart. If only Mr. Kemp was a dumb stupid man who didn't know or care whether you were worth anything... Well, come on." He opened the gate bravely, but he felt shy and unimportant.

"Hello, son. What's on your mind?" Mr. Kemp called from the veranda. He had on a tan-colored shirt, and his gray, untidy moustache was twitching as if the sight of the hesitant boy and dog amused him. The brown skin on his face, now that he was smiling, was more lined and wrinkled and leathery than ever.

"Could I speak to you a minute, Mr. Kemp?" Luke asked solemnly when they were close to the veranda.

"Sure, go ahead, Luke," Mr. Kemp said. His eyes were friendly and amused.

"Well, it's about Dan, Mr. Kemp."

"What about Dan?" Mr. Kemp asked, making a little noise with his fingers that brought Dan up on the veranda and beside him.

"Well, Dan's a great dog, Mr. Kemp, and I guess you know that as well as I do. So I was wondering if you could keep him here for me?"

"Why should I keep Dan here, son?"

"Well, it's like this," Luke said, fumbling the words awkwardly. "My uncle won't let me keep him any more... says he's too old. Of course, he's my uncle's dog, not mine."

As his mouth began to tremble, he blurted out, "They tried to drown Dan, Mr. Kemp."

"They did? Who did? When?"

"This afternoon. That awful old man, Sam Carter, who works for my uncle. Of course he was only doing what my uncle told him to do."

"And how is it they couldn't drown him?"

"I was hiding there. I saw it."

"Well ... ?"

"After old Sam Carter had gone I jumped in."

"Well, well, well. Yes, you would, Luke. Didn't anybody see you?"

"No."

"Oh, I see. I see," Mr. Kemp said softly, and he was looking at Luke with a beautiful old smile full of loving compassion. "And just fancy. There's your Uncle Henry thinking the dog is dead, eh?"

"I guess he does, Mr. Kemp."

"Well, well, well, Luke," Mr. Kemp said, half to himself, and then he was silent and he didn't even look at Luke or the dog, but went on staring across the lake at the pinkish light from the last rays of the setting sun which were touching the grayish line between the sky and the water. And as Luke waited, he grew more despondent, for Mr. Kemp at that moment seemed incapable of the kind of decisive action that would impress Uncle Henry.

"Look here, son," Mr. Kemp said suddenly. "You'd like to keep the dog here, wouldn't you?"

"I sure would, Mr. Kemp," Luke said eagerly.

"But there's a catch in that, Luke. If the dog stayed here, even if I offered to take the dog off your uncle's hands, this would become his home and he would become my dog."

"Well, even at that..."

"I'd be feeding him every day. A dog is loyal to the one who feeds him, do you see, Luke?"

"But Dan would be here, Mr. Kemp."

Then Mr. Kemp got up and came over to the step where Luke had been standing, and he sat down and stroked the collie's head. "Of course, Dan's an old dog, son," he said quietly, "and sooner or later a man has to get rid of an old dog. Your uncle knows that, and maybe it's true that Dan isn't worth his keep any more."

"But he doesn't eat so much, Mr. Kemp," Luke protested. "Just one meal a day."

"I wouldn't want you to think your uncle is cruel and unfeeling, Luke," Mr. Kemp said. "No, I mean that, Luke," he insisted. "Your uncle's a fine man." As the glum despairing expression on the boy's face deepened, Mr. Kemp went on, "Maybe he's a little bit too practical and straightforward. Maybe so intent on seeing what's directly ahead of him that he never takes times to look to the right or the left. Maybe there are valuable things in the world he has no time to look at, things that are more important than anything else to an old man like me or a boy like you. However, the plain truth is that to your uncle the dog isn't worth his keep."

"Yeah. That's it, Mr. Kemp."

"But to you he may be a very valuable dog, eh, Luke?"

"He certainly is, Mr. Kemp."

"Even if you can't explain why to your uncle."

"That's it. I wouldn't make sense, Mr. Kemp," Luke said as he waited, trusting the expression in the old man's eyes.

"Maybe you should make him a practical proposition, Luke."

"I—I don't know what you mean."

"Well, I sort of like the way you get the cows for me in the evenings," Mr. Kemp said, smiling to himself. "In fact, I don't think you need me to go along with you at all. Now, supposing I gave you seventy-five cents a week. Would you get the cows for me every night?"

"Sure, I would, Mr. Kemp. I like doing it, anyway."

"All right, son. It's a deal. Now I'll tell you what to do. You go back to your uncle, and before he has a chance to open up on you, you say right out that you've come to him with a business proposition. Say it like a man, just like that. Offer to pay him the seventy-five cents a week for the dog's keep."

"But my uncle doesn't need seventy-five cents, Mr. Kemp," Luke said uneasily.

"Of course not," Mr. Kemp agreed. "It's the principle of the thing. Be confident. Remember that he's got nothing against the dog. Go to it, son. Let me know how you do," he added, with an amused smile. "If I know your uncle at all, I think it'll work."

"Well..." Luke began doubtfully.

"Go on. Hop to it, Luke."

"Maybe I should leave Dan here, and I should go back and talk to Uncle Henry first."

"Oh, no, Luke. You've got to have a little confidence in your business proposition. Have the dog there with you. It'll be more impressive."

"But if it doesn't work, I'll be handing the dog right back to Uncle Henry. Shucks, Mr. Kemp, it's an awful chance to take. If I could only leave Dan here..."

"If you left Dan here, Luke, I don't think Uncle Henry would have the same respect for you."

"What if he just grabs Dan?"

"You're forgetting he's a practical man and such men always listen to propositions. They don't lose their heads. Have all the confidence in the world, Luke, and the chances are your Uncle Henry will respect you."

"Maybe, but I wish—"

"Go on now, son."

"I'll try it, Mr. Kemp," Luke said. "Thanks very much." But he didn't have any confidence, for even though he knew that Mr. Kemp was a wise man who would not deceive him, he couldn't believe that seventy-five cents a week would stop a man like his uncle. "Come on, Dan," he called, and he went slowly and apprehensively back to the house.

When they were going up the path, his aunt cried from the open window, "Henry, Henry, in heaven's name, it's Luke with the dog."

Ten paces from the veranda, Luke stopped and waited nervously for his uncle to come out. Uncle Henry came out in a rush, but when he saw the collie and Luke standing there, he stopped stiffly and turned pale, and his mouth hung open loosely.

"Luke," he whispered, "that dog had a stone around his neck."

"I fished him out of the stream," Luke said uneasily.

"Oh. Oh, I see," Uncle Henry said. His tone expressed his sudden relief. It was as if he was grateful for the simple explanation which made the world solid and rational again. Gradually the color came back to his face but for a few moments he couldn't speak; his emotion was bewilderingly unfamiliar. He was suddenly so powerfully aware of Luke that he felt embarrassed. He began to struggle to adjust himself to this new awareness or at least to brush it aside quickly before it could disturb his life. "You fished him out, eh?" he asked, still looking at the dog uneasily. "You shouldn't have done that. I told Sam Carter to get rid of him."

"Just a minute, Uncle Henry," Luke said, trying not to falter. He gained confidence as Aunt Helen came out and stood beside her husband, for her eyes seemed to be gentle, and he went on bravely. "I want to make you a practical proposition, Uncle Henry."

"A what?" Uncle Henry asked, still feeling insecure, and wishing the boy and the dog weren't confronting him.

"A practical proposition," Luke blurted out quickly. "I know Dan isn't worth his keep to you. I guess he isn't worth anything to anybody but me. So I'll pay you seventy-five cents a week for his keep."

"What's this?" Uncle Henry asked, looking bewildered. "Where would you get seventy-five cents a week, Luke?"

"I'm going to get the cows every night for Mr. Kemp."

"Oh, for heaven's sake, Henry," Aunt Helen pleaded.

Then she grew flustered and began to make frantic motions with her hands. She couldn't bear the expression in the boy's eyes; it made her feel ashamed and guilty, and then, after the first moment, strangely lonely, and the power of this loneliness which distressed her terribly had to be broken. "Henry," she blurted out desperately, "let him keep the dog," and she fled into the house.

"None of that kind of talk," Uncle Henry called after her. "We've got to be sensible about this." But he was shaken himself, and overwhelmed with a distress that destroyed all his confidence. As he sat down slowly in the rocking chair and stroked the side of his big face, he wanted to say weakly, "All right, keep the dog," but he was ashamed of being so weak and sentimental. He stubbornly refused to yield to this emotion; he was trying desperately to turn his emotion into a bit of good, useful common sense, so he could justify his distress. So he rocked and pondered. At last he smiled. "You're a smart little shaver, Luke," he said slowly. "Imagine you working it out like this. I'm tempted to accept your proposition."

"Why, thanks, Uncle Henry."

"I'm accepting it because I think you'll learn something out of this," he went on ponderously.

"Yes, Uncle Henry."

"You'll learn that useless luxuries cost the smartest of men hard-earned money."

"I don't mind."

"Well, it's a thing you'll have to learn sometime. I think you'll learn, too, because you certainly seem to have a practical streak in you. It's a streak I like to see in a boy. Okay, son," he said, and he smiled with relief and went inside.

Turning to Dan, Luke whispered softly, "Well, what do you know about that?"

As he sat down on the step with the collie beside him and listened to Uncle Henry talking to his wife, he began to glow with exultation. Then gradually his exultation began to change to a vast wonder that Mr. Kemp should have had such a perfect understanding of Uncle Henry. He began to dream of some day being as wise as old Mr. Kemp and knowing exactly how to handle people.

Already he felt years older. Not months but years could have passed since he came to the mill. It seemed to him that he had already learned the most important things about his uncle that his father had wanted him to learn.

In the world there were probably millions of people like Uncle Henry who were kind and strong and because of their strength of character and shrewdness, dominated and flattened out the lives of others. Yet it was possible not only to protect yourself against such people but also to win their respect. It all depended on the weapons you used. If you knew how to handle yourself, there were fascinating ways of demanding respect for the things that gave your own life a secret glow.

Putting his head down on the dog's neck, he vowed to himself fervently that he would always have some money on hand, no matter what became of him, so that he would be able to protect all that was truly valuable from the practical people in the world.